Interior Designed By

1st Edition

ISBN: 978-1-964324-03-6

The Secret Obsession of Clara Wood

By

Candace Meredith

'

Chapter One

The blood seeped from her lip onto the dry cloth.

"What happened, honey?" her husband said from FaceTime on her phone, as she moved swiftly to the standing mirror.

She was staying at the cabin her mother left her. Nestled deeply in the woods of Vermont, her mother's family cabin was covered in an oasis of shrubbery. Her mother loved to tend to the garden.

"Bit my own lip like it was a candy bar."

She had told her husband she'd be at the cabin on weekends where she could do her painting. Her mother put her through art school before Parkinson's disease riddled her body; then the dementia took her mind too.

"Who are you, dear?" her mother would say to her from behind a starchy white bedsheet at the hospital; she loved begonias and lavender. She'd remember that too, momentarily, along with her daughter's name on days she could wheel her mother through the garden.

Her mother would recall a memory triggered by the scent of flowers.

"What's your name?" another man's voice whispered from behind the mirror, as her mind snapped back to reality. She quickly muted her FaceTime call so her husband wouldn't hear, and discretely tilted her phone screen away from her face, so her husband wouldn't see.

"It's Clara," she told the man.

"Do you have a last name, Clara?"

"It's Wood," she said before unmuting the FaceTime call from her end.

"I'll be coming home," she said subtly and ended the call.

Her husband was always busy. He ran a hotel that he owned, among other luxuries, and Clara had inherited the cabin. When she changed her name from Wood to Newman she felt a kind of disconnect from her mother but the name her mother gave her was from a man she could never relate with. Her mother had a disconnect herself from the name – the name she inherited but no father, and then later from her husband, ever gave her a name of honor.

"And what's yours?" she asked the man. She took a bite of a juicy, ripened strawberry, but the sweetness of the succulent fruit burned her damaged lip a little.

"I'm sorry about that," he said and lightly touched her bottom lip with a moistened cloth.

"A name..."

She wasn't exactly into subtleties.

"It's Hunter." His deep, chocolate, almond-like eyes bore a hole in her skin.

"Just Hunter?"

"Green."

"Hunter Green, like the color?"

"That's right," he said with a toothy grin.

4

Clara ate another strawberry. He applied the whipped cream, and she sucked at the bits on his finger.

"My wet cloth is better than your dry cloth," he teased her.

"Being dry isn't my thing," she said, poking fun back.

"I can't say I'd like you being dry Clara..." He ran his hand up her thigh. "I'd love to make you wet like a good ole boy."

Clara liked his accent. He was from the Bronx, but Clara had asked only a few questions when they met on her front stoop.

She'd thought he was a would-be squatter, but he turned out to be a hiker, a passerby on his way through Vermont.

Their initial conversation had ended abruptly due to their chemistry.

"You're alone in the cabin?" He loved her body.

"Are you going to kill me?" She toyed with him.

"I don't kill a thing."

"You never killed a big old buck?"

"Never shot one in my life." He smiled and she wiped a sliver of mayo from his lip like he did for her blood that left her lip puffy.

They were forceful in the bedroom. He stroked her hair hard as he slowly penetrated her half naked, ravished body from behind.

He loved her. He took from her all she had because she'd given to him her everything. He knew it. She knew it too. They didn't have to say a word. Their pants were rattled at the ankle when they went through the front door.

5

The painting she did of her mother had eyes upon them.

"She's looking …" he said, and she tossed her jean jacket upon the canvas, and he took her by the hair and forced her onto the bed.

She gasped and grabbed at the sheet with her left hand.

He bore into her so deep she almost cried. She was subdued, like really being wanted. He used his tongue where she couldn't be penetrated so he could arouse in her something primal.

She wanted him back. She wanted, thirsted, and craved being craved.

"Hunter is a proud name," she said afterward, and in that moment she could have lit a cigarette if she hadn't given it up.

"My daddy's name," he said with a kind of innocence that made him sexier.

In the bed, before the name exchange, they had lapped at one another's bodies like a dog does for water after the heat.

The heat in the bedroom was smoking hard, and when he pulled her hair back, she moaned into the pillow she was grasping. He ravished her like that in the one room cabin. She thought she saw the ghost of her mother for a moment peering through the window; then she realized her mother couldn't be there then, because her mother quit smoking too. When the image of her mother lit a smoke outside the window, Clara paused and rolled her eyes.

"She always came to this cabin without my daddy." She was equally coy.

"Who?"

"My mother."

"The painting?"

"Yeah."

She popped open the wine bottle and poured another glass. This was their second time in the cabin together. This was their first night to become Clara Wood and Hunter Green. They liked it in that moment to know one another by a name. A name of someone, something, that made them thirsty.

The second time, when he threw her into the bed, her lip hit the wooden frame.

Clara had been attending the cabin since her mother, Norma Jean Haywood, died. Her mother, named decidedly after the famous one, and previously Wood until she met her husband, had chuckled over the Wood and Haywood coincidence. Clara laughed in the mix of memory and desire.

She settled with the fact that she could not have her mother but could have her passion. They both had a passion for art. They both were eccentric—her mother in an earthy way, and Clara in an eclectic way. She was dark. Her mother had the light in her. Clara admired that. She missed her mother greatly. They were best friends. Clara uncovered her mother's portrait when Hunter went out for a walk barefoot on the porch. It was freezing.

"Feels good on my feet," he said, and she thought then about their first night in the cabin. They were on her front stoop where she found him when she made the drive in her Discovery. She thought he must be a squatter. The place was remote. He had bare feet then, too, so she knew she had something different before her; even the air was different. There was a good deal of puffy, dark cloud cover and mist, but something more omnipresent felt present around them. She was awed. Subdued by him. Her senses were fully aroused being restrained by him and as her depression grew, she felt a deeper connection to him. His thirst for her body made her heart go wild.

The eyes of her mother never left her like her father had; by the time she was six, her father left a battered woman and their child. Her mother explained they'd both be dead if he stayed. The man with no name, other than their shared sentiments over the coincidence of their last names, was a kind of dark cloud to Clara. She thought about how her mother took the last name of a father who was never there, then a last name of another who also would never be there. Wood was her mother's maiden name and Clara received the name in spite of the bastard who gave her a child. He hit her eventually over that, even though the first time he left was when she was pregnant, and she gave birth alone. Norma was haunted when he came back and never knew how to love or be loved. Not from her drunken father nor her abusive husband.

He stayed etched in Clara's paint as a man with no name. That name died with her mother. Norma preferred to address him the only occasion they discussed him as "that man." Because that was all he would ever be.

Norma stayed quiet, reclusive, and afraid. She raised her daughter alone out of preference, and Clara got a public-school education in West Virginia. They lived in a tiny little bungalow on the farm where her mother worked. She loved horses. But she also taught Clara how to paint—a gift Norma received by her mother who taught her when she was, herself, a child.

Norma's mother, Helen, used pastels and oils on canvas, which was Clara's preferred medium; Helen learned from her mother, Lucille, and Norma often explained their long lineage of giftedness in the arts.

Clara had those portraits too; her mother kept them privately contained in a pink box atop her closet. They were passed down to Clara upon her death. Clara knew it was all her mother possessed because she worked the horse stables for food and boarding. It was in a quiet, quaint little town called Capon Bridge, and Clara enjoyed the river as a child. She collected salamanders and minnows.

Then her mother told her about a cabin in Vermont. Clara had never been, and Norma never mentioned it until she heard about the death of "that man." Norma was too afraid to go there in fear of his finding them, so Norma only took her daughter when she felt safer in the world.

That cabin became a weekend trip. Norma kept a tiny little car like she did a tiny little house, but that blue Versa was hers; the bungalow was home, but the cabin was refuge and would be for Clara too. Within that cabin they painted. It was when Clara turned eighteen that she excelled and painted her mother's portrait in oils and used acrylic, which was also a medium she preferred. Her mother's portrait remained unfinished on the easel because her mother liked it unfinished. She didn't want too much detail like the lines in her cheeks, the creases under her eyes or the way the skin under her chin sagged a little.

Clara turned twenty-two and Norma began with Parkinson's, then five years later the dementia, and five years after that, Clara would bury Norma.

At thirty-two, the same year as her mother's death, she met Hunter Green. At twenty-two, she had met Quinton Newman and two years later they married. At thirty she thought she had it all; then her mother began to only know her name subtly at times through paint; the Parkinson's riddled the bones in her hands and her joints and Norma lost all memories of her daughter, and Clara fell ill from the death of her mother.

She wasn't sure what saved her when her mother died because she should have died too.

Clara was hospitalized and induced in a coma to bring her back from the brink of death after she contacted malaria from the toxic water she drank abroad, because she thought a trip to England would invoke in her a sense of life again. But Clara couldn't breathe; she constantly felt the sensation of drowning taking her breaths away, and she fled to the cabin.

The cabin was never the same. And neither was her life.

She met Quinton at the art gallery. She won a trip to New York City where she was invited to showcase their art. Clara scheduled the visit as a surprise for her mother. The dementia would be diagnosed years later, but the Parkinson's was that year, and the art gallery would remain a vivid memory for Clara. The gallery owner personally responded to her inquiry to showcase four generations of art. She was scheduled to showcase her art the following year after her initial inquiry.

"Mom, I'm taking you to New York," she said in the bungalow.

Clara stayed with her mother after she had been diagnosed with Parkinson's.

"New York?" Her expression was perplexed.

"Yes."

"What for?"

"It's a surprise."

"Well, I don't really know if I'll like it."

Her mother was beautiful. She had striking black hair and dark eyes. Her skin shone dark too and Clara loved the nude tones of her mother's complexion. She felt that portrait was what captivated the owner most.

He would in fact ask about that portrait at the gallery.

"She's a beautiful artist," her mother said inside the gallery, "but not the model so much." She blushed.

"Nonsense." The gallery owner, Paul, nudged her chin. Paul's partner in life and in work, Thomas, was equally stellar and the two of them set up the display amid a busy day in New York when a nearby talent agency was putting out a free, walk-in talent request. The show brought in thousands, but all this was to be a surprise for Norma, and Clara only told her that she had won a trip to the city, as they called it.

Clara arrived at the hotel in New York where Paul booked her reservations. Norma was overwhelmed but she maintained composure for her daughter who set up the whole affair. Her hands shook and she was wheel-chaired around often because her body felt weak, but she walked on occasion when she could, especially at home in the garden. But the city was a different ballgame entirely. Norma almost had tears in her eyes from the commotion over them when they arrived at the gallery the following morning.

"Mom," Clara whispered, "they wanted our art."

The gallery was beyond beautiful; the extravagance was exhilarating because Norma loved fine crystal and the chandeliers were exquisite.

"Our art?" she gasped.

Clara showcased their art in one of the finest art galleries in New York City and Norma about fell over.

They were simple, ordinary folk in her mind and Clara really outdid herself. There were oil paintings of roses from Helen's garden, which Helen painted in exquisite detail as if the rose was amplified against a world of light; Norma felt that her mother was ahead of her time. She was a brilliant woman who also loved to read. Norma could write stories beginning in kindergarten and was also a prodigy in the classroom. Clara excelled in courses and fell in love with photography because the display in the other showcase room was from local photographer James Morrison. James had a sister, Ashley Baldwin, and her husband had a brother named Quinton Newman. They were brothers of the same mother but had different fathers since she re-married and had Quinton ten years before her second son, Vincent (Vinny), was born. Vincent Baldwin and his wife, Ashley, attended the show to support James. Clara always loved photography and decided to pry into the show in the next room. She wheeled her mother around the pillars containing enlarged images and came upon a portrait of a man wearing a costume: The photo bore the name Quinton Newman. He had a physique of a model and a strapping guitar.

"He looks like Elvis..." Clara began when a man commented from behind.

"Everyone tells him that," James said, and Clara and her mother spun around to find James standing in a dark suit. His wife, Mystique, joined them; she was radiant with dark skin in a light dress. Clara thought she looked like a model herself and reminded her of a radiant goddess the stories were told about.

"Halloween 1999," Mystique said, and her amber eyes shown compassion.

"We were attending a party." James smiled with a bit of coolness in his swag, and Clara beamed. Norma loved Elvis since her mother loved him so much, and every Christmas they played songs written by Elvis. Mystique walked closer to the portrait and pointed. "It's done in black and white. I'm surprised you didn't think he was Elvis." She laughed.

"James is too young to know Elvis, my daughter." Norma laughed in a high-pitched bellow and tapped Clara on the back as if saying to find out more.

As shown in the photo, Quinton was a tan version of Elvis. Clara didn't really know what to say so she went with the obvious. "What kind of party?"

"My bachelor party actually." James laughed.

"Well, is he married?" Norma cut right to it.

"No. He's kinda shy." James seemed to be more reserved than his wife.

"Quinton loves art," Mystique said.

"My sister's husband's brother..." James started, trying to explain.

"Quinton." Mystique was someone who easily could have all the attention at the party.

"We're all very close," James said.

"How long have you been doing photography?" Clara asked.

"For as long as I can remember. My grandfather was a photographer, and I learned from him."

"I learned art, how to paint, from my mother. Then mom worked a second job and helped me with art school." Clara placed her hands to her mother's shoulders.

"It was only a two-year program. We couldn't afford much." Norma was being modest but to Clara she was an angel.

"I'm sorry. I didn't think to ask your names…" James reminded them.

"Well, I am Norma," she said.

Clara was more reserved, and they shook her hand gracefully.

Mystique's fingers were soft. Her nails manicured in red.

"I recognized your portrait from the galley next door," James said.

"Yes…" Norma began.

"We are here with four generations of art," Clara piped in.

"Four generations of women?" Mystique said.

"That's right," Norma said with a nod, and Clara tried to peek at the exhibit next door in which a large crowd was mingling.

"It's looking busy for you," James said with a glance over his shoulder, "but if you ever want to meet Elvis, here's my card." He flashed her a personal business card alongside a slick grin.

"He means if you would like to meet up, artist to artist, then reach out any time." Mystique waved gently as they greeted other guests and James tugged at his sister's shoulder while she mingled among the guests.

"My sister would love to see your art," James politely said.

"Ashley dotes on artists." Her husband, Vincent, smiled.

"This is Elvis's brother, Vinny." Ashley laughed.

"My brother got all of his good looks from our mother."

"And what is your mother's name?"

"It's Athena."

"Like a goddess..." Clara really did like mythology.

"Yes." Vinny was spectacular despite his non-Elvis looks. He did, however, have a winning personality.

Chapter Two

Athena wore long dresses. Always long dresses. She was stylish, exquisite and she owned the best five-star hotel New York had to offer. She was the mother of Quinton Newman and Vincent Baldwin. Vinny, ten years younger than Quinton, came as a surprise during her second marriage when she thought she could not have any more babies. Vinny and Quinton lived lavishly as children of a highly successful mother who tended all business matters regarding the estate she owned when she met second husband, Nathaniel Baldwin. Quinton called his stepfather Nate the Dogg, and they laughed at that often; he was always on the prowl for good investments. Nathaniel owned several casinos around Atlanta and liked to gamble. He'd bet on horse races and gambled over the stock market. Athena met her match in respect to sharing the wealth of prosperity they each offered in the marriage. Quinton's father, Richard Newman, was a wealthy tobacco factory owner. He had stocks and investments in real estate, and he binged on capitalizing in insurance. Athena left wealth for wealth when she simply stated she grew apart from her first husband. He took the real estate and she had the hotel. Hotel Athena was grand, and New York was bustling with tourists who found the accommodations pleasing, especially the rooftop pool, outdoor bar, spa, and sauna. The hotel offered a resort-like feature in the city.

Clara would meet Quinton Newman after the gallery. Athena was having brunch with a friend and stopped by the gallery to shed their love and support for James, whose photography appeared aside Clara and Norma's art. Being Ashley's mother-in-law, Athena felt she could further James's reputation. Athena had a way with elites and felt James could use the reputation elevation.

"James, you capture an exquisite angle on light off ice."

"Thank you, Athena darling." He doted on her. He kissed her left cheek.

Clara had never been around extreme wealth.

"Meet the artists from the gallery room," James said, and Athena turned subtly.

"James captures light off ice like my mother painted rose petals." Norma thought highly of her mother's talents.

Athena looked to the showcase, and through the opening she could see precisely the oil on canvas Norma referred to.

"Will it appreciate?" It was natural for Athena to think of money.

"It already has dear." Norma smiled.

"Surely." Athena gave her a nod.

Ashley piped in for the first time. "Well, what did you paint?"

Clara could tell that Ashley thought highly of them. She was sweet and bounced lightly on her toes when she walked. Ashley was not from wealth. Her own parents worked in the auto business, her father as a service writer and her mother as an accountant; they met at the dealership and married a year later. Ashley and Vinny were quick to marry, three months after they met, and Vinny knew not to let his mother get a word in. Her oldest son, however, was not married, and Ashley thought she saw potential from the offset; Clara had a talent for art like her own mother and they were not from wealth, also making Ashley more comfortable in their presence.

"We think the young man in the portrait looks like Elvis." Norma didn't let upbringing come between her and a good conversation.

17

"He does. My ex-husband did also." Athena was eyeing the art.

"But your son said…" Norma began.

"That he gets all his good looks from his mother," she laughed subtly. "He always says that. Being simple I guess." She marveled and continued, "Couldn't sing worth a darn." Athena laughed lightly and her smile shone healthy white teeth. Clara thought they looked like porcelain.

"The young woman in the portrait looks like Lucille Ball, doesn't she?" Athena said to her family.

"That's my mother," Norma explained. "She had red hair and kept it nicely tied back. With a ribbon in her youth and a bun as she grew older."

Athena's hair had a natural gray tone to her blond tresses that were pulled into a fashionable French roll with a twist.

Norma had long locks of straight dark hair that glowed with strands of gray like accents. Clara thought her mother's hair was like silk. She kept a shorter bobbed do and had chunky highlights.

Athena walked toward the painting of rose petals that were the color of her nails. "I'll take this one," she said. "I have a new hotel going up, and I'll hang this one in the lobby." She looked proud.

"What hotel?" Clara was sweet.

"In New Jersey." Her answer was short.

"She wants to know if it has a name." Norma was frank.

"Hotel Athena." Athena snorted when she laughed, and her speech was a bit nasally.

"It will look beautiful there," Ashley said, and she eyed James who was taken by a browser who wanted photography for his chiropractic office.

Clara and Norma were invited to dine with Ashley and Vinny in their home. Ashley loved to cook, and she had a plan. Ashley liked to cook Italian food and Vinny enjoyed pasta dishes. He told Clara she would really enjoy being around Ashley because her energy was high; while he was low he had Ashley.

"Being raised by Athena wasn't the easiest," he confided privately at the gallery. Athena had already walked off to mingle and get James the best dollar. Ashley liked Athena, but their energy and their nature was different. Ashley helped Vinny overcome the trauma of always trying to earn money, which both his parents loved, and he found through her a way into loving life outside of wealth. He had the commodities: the wave runners, paddle boards, snow skis, and every brand of shoes for every sport. Ashley had the wealth of love in her background. Her parents always earned enough, and she grew up feeling safe. "That was important," she said to him on their first date, "because I know the world can be a scary place." He told bits and pieces to Clara, but he wanted them to get to know one another, "because an artist is right up her alley."

Secretly they wanted Quinton to meet a nice woman who wasn't trying to marry into money and Clara struck them as earnest. "I have a good feeling about her," Ashley told him in their private conversation in the corner. At the end of the day and when the gallery was due to close, Ashley gave Clara her number and address. "Do I need to bring anything?" Clara felt awkward. "Just your best dress." Ashley laughed in a little whimper that was almost like a sneeze.

"Okay." Clara looked to Norma who winked.

19

They were able to sell five of their own paintings that evening, and they split the cash by fifty percent, giving them each five thousand dollars.

"I wonder why they were willing to pay so much," Clara said of their buyers.

"Because they are works of original art and you never know," she said, giving her daughter a nudge. "Maybe they'll be worth more when we're dead." Norma laughed.

The unsold paintings would be going home with them that following Monday, but Clara first bought a nice black dress with sequins that was form fitting and comfortable at the same time along with strappy little heels to match. She then purchased a clutch purse and red roses. She felt ready in time to dine at Vinny and Ashley's lovely little studio apartment that was across the street from Central Park. Upon knocking at the front door, she heard a dog barking, and when Vinny answered, he found her exquisitely dressed; though, based on his attire, she wondered if she overdressed.

"Oh," she said, "I took you literally..."

"As you should have." He chuckled and extended his arm for her to swiftly move inside.

She found Ashley who was dining in a red satin dress, and she felt relief.

"You look gorgeous," Ashley said, and Clara was thankful. They were a few years apart in age, but both felt appropriate around one another.

"Quinton is fashionably late," Vinny said and plucked a canapé from the tray.

"More so than your attire." She kissed him.

They had cheese and wine and tidbits of pastries all prepared by Ashley.

"I love to cook," she said as Clara looked about the kitchen island that was visible to the open living space.

Their apartment was small, but Ashley told her they would be taking dinner out to the terrace that overlooked the city.

"I thought this was better than letting Ashley set you up on a blind date," Vinny whispered and stole another canapé before the knock at the door.

"We can go out the terrace." Ashley took her by the arm and they ascended to the rooftop that overlooked the Big Apple.

"It's best for them to mingle it over," Ashley said, and Clara wondered why she hadn't said "ponder it over."

"So he doesn't know I'm here?" she said, and Ashley handed her an empty glass.

"Merlot or Champagne?"

"Merlot." Clara preferred dry wine.

Ashley filled her glass as the men joined them outside. "Well, he does now."

"Ladies." Vinny was chill.

"This is Quinton, Vinny's older brother." Ashley beat him to the punch.

"You had to throw older into it?" Quinton was charming.

21

Clara thought how winning a trip to New York resulted in more than she could ever have imagined. She wondered how her mother was doing in the hotel; Norma did not attend because her grown daughter needed to be a woman on her own. Clara didn't mind. She was assertive enough and outgoing. Quinton gave her a warm handshake and she felt almost lost in his presence in the moment because there she was with a man who wasn't just in the top ranks of prosperity but also resembled Elvis. She was really taken aback.

"Hello," she said sweetly, and Quinton popped the next question.

"Can I fix you a mixed drink?"

"I'd love a margarita. Mango, sugar on the rim. No salt."

"Doesn't salt go with tequila?"

"No." She was mightier than the sword. "Only with my lemon drop shooter."

"Vodka?"

"Definitely."

He shrugged.

He made a margarita from the bar and a shot of vodka Grey Goose with a salted lemon on the side.

"Seriously, though,"—he wasn't letting this one go—"isn't it usually the other way around?"

"Yes." She laughed. "But salt ruins the mango."

"Ah," he said, "but why salt with the shot of vodka?"

"Salt doesn't ruin the lemon. But I'll take it either way."

"The salt or the sugar?"

"Exactly."

"I'll do sugar next time."

"If you prefer."

She took the shot and he doubled back to take a brief glimpse of her ass before he offered her the lemon to follow the vodka. Clara wasn't thick but she wasn't missing out on having an ass. They took a seat at the table made entirely of glass and Clara placed a red cloth napkin across her lap. Ashley served Italian garlic knots and pasta: a baked penne with three cheeses and garnished with green onion and chives. She was able to taste a hint of rosemary and liked the flavor. The pasta was beautifully done with a thin crust of baked cheese and a side of fresh green salad with baby spinach and romaine hearts. The vinaigrette dressing tasted sweet to counteract the earlier dry wine; all the flavors seemed to come together other than her mango, which was a passion fruit and more advantageous than pasta. She felt like she should be at a party for Mardi Gras but she liked the margarita to complement the weather. It was a warm day in July and Ashley situated them for a surprise display of fireworks that could be seen over the city.

The first crack from the explosion of indigo was a vibrant display like a huge star over the balcony.

"I never knew they had fireworks in the city."

Quinton laughed. "Where are you from?"

"The country."

"What part of the country?"

"I'm from a small town in West Virginia."

"How small?"

"Two hundred people?"

Clara wasn't really sure, but she felt the number was fair enough.

"And now you're venturing toward, what? About eight million?"

"I won a trip here to New York."

"What for?"

"To host my art. I applied online and I won the contest."

"They liked your art the best?"

"She did just say she won the contest." Ashley giggled.

"It appears they did."

"Tell him about the four generations." James was casual and cool.

"Yes, my mother's art, and her mother's art and then her mother as well…"

"Hence the four generations." Quinton was quick.

"That's right."

"Nice. And which generation painted the best?"

"My mother would say her mother."

"What would you say?"

"I'd say my mother…"

"But she learned from your grandmother." James was also quick.

"Exactly."

"Who learned from her own mother."

"Yes." Clara was enjoying the conversation. "My mother, Norma, learned from the best! Helen," Clara continued, "learned from Lucille and I think the lineage stops there."

"It's a tremendous accomplishment for a woman that long ago, I think?" James said.

"Definitely," Ashley replied. "Women were never expected to do much."

"My father played the piano," Quinton added to the conversation.

"Richard plays piano?" James was inquisitive.

Mystique mingled aside him near the balcony where the fireworks display was most visible.

"Played the piano. When he was younger."

"Why did he give it up?"

"It died with his youth I guess." Quinton shrugged.

"Well fortunately not all things disappeared like the piano."

"Like what?"

"His good looks." James bashed his brother-in-law often and Quinton never thought to feel smug around him. Their musings were all in good fun.

"He does have a point," Ashley said between sips of plush rose-colored wine.

"That's what the generations had to pass down I guess." Quinton raised his glass to toast, and they all boasted.

"To passing on good genes," Ashley marveled.

"To many more blessings to follow," James said, and Clara looked to Quinton with a sideways glance and she could see he hadn't taken his eyes off of her.

Chapter Three

Clara was due to return home the next day. She knew she'd be too far from Quinton, and she talked subtly with Norma over breakfast on the balcony of the resort-like hotel. The accommodations included meals, and they felt powerful as punch having the $5k in their pockets. Other than art, Clara's vocation consisted of making wages at the bank. The neighborhood bank hosted the nicest and friendliest people, and she spoke of having a nice, simple life in the country.

"But you always have the cabin," her mother said.

Clara hadn't thought of that.

"You can have your man and your art."

"And my mom." Clara loved her mother.

They shared a bond as a pair because Clara was an only child.

She felt like they could never be broken.

"She said we could be like sisters."

"Who?"

"Ashley."

"The sister she never had I guess."

"I guess."

"Is she not close with Mystique?"

"James and Mystique stay busy, she said."

"Doesn't everybody?"

"Sure. Most do I suppose."

"Mystique was glamorous."

"Ashley was exquisite too but at a different level."

"That's it then. Their personalities are different."

"Vinny says he was saved by her."

"Why did he need saving?"

"Drugs. Alcohol."

"And you all were drinking?"

"I know."

"Is it still a problem?"

"He didn't say it was."

"Maybe he just liked to party a little too much."

"They seem settled."

"Then that answers the question."

They sipped coffee. Ate muffins and biscuits and blueberries. They had crepes with butter and strawberry drizzle; they were in hog Heaven. The day was nearing noon when Quinton sent her a text:

Any time for tea?

He added a cute little emoji.

And crumpets? she texted back.

If you're British, he wrote back with a laughing emoji, and she snickered.

"What?" her mother said.

"He wants to have tea."

"Oh, you two go for it. I'm too old for this."

"You're only sixty-two."

"Shouldn't have waited 'til I was thirty-nine to get knocked up."

"You didn't know, Mom."

"I should have. He was my father all over again."

"Forgive him?"

"I moved on long ago."

"Literally, we moved on."

"We did." She gave her daughter a hug.

"Do you mind the age gap?" Clara wanted her mother's opinion.

Clara felt her mother might say something to that effect.

"It's only nine years. The same as me and your father."

"You've never said that before."

"I told you he was older."

"No, you never called him a father."

"That's because he wasn't one."

"Why should that change now?"

"No reason. Wasn't thinking."

Her mother stood up and went to the bathroom to wash.

"You're walking today."

"These old legs work on occasion."

Clara met Quinton at a nearby cafe for tea. Turned out he wasn't kidding. He liked tea in place of coffee, on occasion. He had hot green tea served with pastries and a cup of chili since he thought the time called for lunch.

"Does your mother already not like me?" he snarled at seeing her walk in alone.

"No. She hates all men." She meant it.

"Well, my mother liked her, and my mother isn't easy to please."

"What else did she say?"

"She said if the art wasn't sold that day, she'd contact a collector she knows, if you're interested."

As James explained in their meeting, it was always business with Athena. Clara took a seat at a modest little table and ordered a grilled sandwich and salad greens.

"How's your head?" he asked.

"My head?"

"Thought you might have awoken with a headache."

"Why?" she sneered. "I didn't drink that much."

She felt cautious in regard to Vinny and his experiences with stimulants and depressants. The crazy combination made her head hurt to think about it; she wondered what Quinton's experience was with the whole situation, and because Vinny had seemed to confide in her, she didn't press the topic. She was also a bit sensitive regarding her mother's experiences; her mother instilled caution into her. She wondered if her drinking bothered her mother, but Norma never said a word. Clara thought about the collector. She knew her mother didn't want to sell all of her mother's art, and together they hadn't thought it all through. The rose petals were Norma's favorite, and she would never have her mother back.

"I don't think we can sell all the art. They're originals and we just didn't think..."

"You didn't think they would sell?"

"No."

"Those paintings sound like precious heirlooms. I'll talk with her, and I'm sure we can help you get prints made."

"Like Dali?"

"Sure, why not?"

She felt very official.

"The money is nice and all…" Clara saw it in her mother's eyes when it dawned on her that they would be leaving without her mother's precious art.

"What the hell was I thinking?" Norma had said with the check in her hand.

"No problem." Quinton was familiar with business and sentiments—a quality Clara ascribed to Ashley. "What time does your plane depart?"

"It's at eight twenty-five this evening."

"Do you want to talk again?"

"We can."

"That's not as promising as a yes."

"Yes." She was smitten, but Clara would never admit to it.

"I really liked Ashley and Vinny." She wanted a conversation that wasn't going South.

"They are good people, my brother and his wife, and they seem to think most women want to use me for money."

"Oh?"

"I hope you don't mind me being frank here…"

"No…"

"I did have some pick-pockets in the past."

"Tell me."

"One of them stole my check book and wrote herself some checks."

"Did you take her to court?"

"Not over a couple grand. Would cost me just as much for an attorney."

"How long ago was she?"

"She was my last relationship."

"You've had many?"

"Here or there."

"What does that mean?"

"I've had some short-term girlfriends, and the relationships never seemed to go anywhere."

"What caused the dead end? More pick-pockets?"

"Not like the last one."

Clara had only been in one relationship so she could not relate. His name was Fernando, and he was a charming Italian who left her for another woman. Clara was twenty at the time, and she didn't date after that. Now, the whole affair with Quinton felt like a journey that told her it was meant to be: He was looking for someone who would not use him for money, and she was looking for someone who would not abandon her. Two years after her other relationship ended, she felt like she was being rescued by Ashley, who felt Clara was someone genuine. Clara enjoyed the idea of being that woman. She thought she could show a man what a real relationship was like. She also contended that she, too, would be learning.

Clara finished her leafy-greens and placed her napkin upon the table. That's when Quinton touched her delicately on the hand and professed, "I'm willing to give this thing a chance if you are." She felt his earnestness and responded, "I am."

She reached Norma back at the hotel lobby where she had access to the WiFi and was finishing up some emails when Clara entered with Quinton; it was the first time she'd get to meet him.

"I sent the last newsletter and I'm ready to go."

"My mother left the stables and teaches preschool children."

Norma didn't look at Quinton.

"Hello ma'am," he said.

"Mom, meet Quinton."

"You're dashing." She winked.

"Thank you..."

"Just like Elvis!"

Norma might have been sold on the idea of his being the spitting image of Elvis. She was named after the glamorous Marilyn Monroe, and she enjoyed taking on the last name of another woman in the limelight. She kept two names from two scrubs as she called them, and she preferred to do away with the ties to any last name. They both had a last name of no significance and that was Norma's mentality regarding men in general. No significance.

"Don't mind my mom," Clara said outside the hotel lobby door.

There were hotel staff assisting them with their luggage.

"A limo?" Norma gasped.

"It's okay, Mom." Clara knew her mother wasn't into being flashy. She was a simple woman.

"Well, you could have called a damn taxicab!" She meant it.

"Nah, they smell too funky," Quinton tried to joke.

"Does this one smell any better?" Norma half joked.

"You'll have to get in and find out."

Norma got in.

"It smells like cow hide."

The leather seats were the color black and the lighting was the color of mauve.

"What's with the lighting in here?" She wasn't considering the whole idea of luxury by way of effects.

Quinton reached over and turned a switch to fluorescent.

"That's better," Norma said, and they departed for the airport.

That night back at home in West Virginia, Norma confided she didn't think he seemed too shabby.

"He's kinda shabby chic," she chided.

"Are you scolding me for that?"

They both got a laugh. Norma could be complicated. Clara blamed it on her past.

"You'll never lose me, Mom." Clara told her mother on their front porch swing; the bungalow was lit with insect repellent burners and the atmosphere had an air of citronella.

"I hope I never do," she told her daughter, and they turned in for the night shortly after.

At early dawn, the sky was purple over the West Virginia mountains. Norma was in her white satin robe having coffee on their porch when Quinton and Clara joined her.

Norma looked disgruntled. "You didn't tell me he'd be coming by."

"Surprise!" Clara was funny.

"I'm in my damn robe."

Quinton was in his boxer briefs. He clearly looked too comfortable.

"When the hell did he get here?"

"After you went to bed, he showed up."

"My flight was cancelled."

"How convenient." Norma sipped her coffee. "This used to be better with a cigarette."

"You used to smoke?"

"We both did until last year." Clara was young, but with Norma working two jobs to get by with a daughter, Clara was left to raise

36

herself most of the time. That's when she got used to being out late, partying, and smoking. She wasn't unfamiliar with wild times, and she felt that kind of connection to Vinny and Ashley. Quinton, in a short amount of time, was growing on her too. He was superbly educated. She liked his know-how regarding the numbers and his brain was like a sponge for the facts. And she was growing on him too.

Chapter Four

She began taking weekend trips to New York while her mother went to the cabin to paint. Clara went to the cabin too on occasion, especially when Quinton was tied up with business affairs. He was employed in marketing for the hotel and used analytics to summarize data. He outsourced the know-how to get a failing company thriving again, and he was good at it. He worked in New York, had a multi-million-dollar apartment fourteen minutes outside of Jersey, and his mother asked him to promote the hotel.

Together, Athena and Quinton generated revenue that meant he could invest in Wall Street. His investments alone made millions, and with that money he invested in a bank. Quite frankly they were a powerhouse. And he wanted a woman. Not a trophy wife who was into stealing his cash. And that woman was Clara. But Clara was certainly a trophy in her own right; she wasn't wealthy, but she was beautiful and so was Norma. Quinton said once that his college buddy told him he could judge a woman by how well her mother looks. Norma aged well and she shined too. Quinton said the pair were a rare gem. They were elegant and classy women who kept their appearance looking sharp and beckoned a kind of respect one feels at being in their presence.

Quinton, then owning the bank, asked Clara if she would like to manage it and move to New York. She wasn't sure how Norma would feel, considering they were only a few months into a long-distance relationship. Clara wanted her mother's blessing and felt only a good man would sway her on the side of acceptance of a man in her daughter's life, since Norma never really had one.

Norma had Helen, and Helen was also married and divorced twice. Those two men were unfaithful and unyielding to showing much love for a woman. Helen died at age eighty after a severe stroke that left Norma nursing her mother at home in hospice. She didn't have money to leave Norma and Clara, but she left them the cabin: a beautiful and quaint little abode with one room and a full bath. "It has running water," Helen joked, "and a pot to piss in." Those were her last words. And she joined Lucille in Heaven. Lucille Eleanor was Helen's mother, and she was a strong woman who was blessed with five babies. Norma's last sister, Betty, died at age sixty-five and was the last surviving offspring. Norma only had her daughter left, and Clara could sense that emotion from her mother.

"I'll never leave you, Mom," she said one day, when the two were visiting the cabin together.

"How is he doing lately?" she asked.

"He's happy. I think."

"You think?"

"From what I can tell."

Norma begun painting peonies that were outside the cabin in full bloom. It was late September, and the weather was still warm.

"It'll be October soon," Clara said. "Our favorite time of year for the harvest season.

Clara had loved October since her youth. She and Norma were not religious and their beliefs were eclectic and varied upon the latest book about energy and the alignment of the planets. Astrology was fun but Clara felt there was more to it than gravity—like forces of interstellar constellations contained within each human.

"We're just a speck," she told Norma when she was reading a good book, "like a tiny microcosm within a strong and powerful macrocosm."

Clara would grow to miss those conversations. Fernando never wanted to entertain her theories on energy being inherent in all living things making all living beings interconnected at a deeply profound level. She couldn't get him to chat over tea like she could with Quinton.

"He told me he wants to come to the cabin sometime," she finally told her mother.

"I'm sorry, but he's not invited. That's why you have New York now."

"But you cannot stay here alone."

"I've already put the house up for sale."

"What? Why?"

"I've been diagnosed with Parkinson's disease." Her mother's eyes didn't leave the paint.

"What? When?"

"Last week."

Clara was staying at the cabin to celebrate her mother's sixty-third birthday.

"Betty's husband passed last week."

"Don't change the subject, Mom."

"Parkinson's disease is a slow process, I have plenty of time."

"Do you?"

"Of course I do."

"I can't leave you alone in this cabin while I'm in New York, Mom."

"Of course you can. What the hell is going to happen?"

"Anything, Mom."

"We have cell phones you know!"

"And barely any service out here."

"I'll be fine."

"Where are you going to stay without the bungalow? And you just sold my home too, you know?"

"But you have New York now."

"Stop saying that, Mom. I know I met a guy, but I still have you too."

"I can afford what little this cabin costs me, and I can finally afford to retire."

"You cannot stay here alone."

"You watch me, love bug." A nickname she ascribed Clara early in youth.

Norma was stern and headstrong.

"Ruby from town will stop in to see me, and I pay her to bring the groceries. Seriously it's the twenty-first century and I'm a grown woman! Think about that."

"But now ... Parkinson's?"

"Slowly degenerative," her mother said with the wave of her hand.

Clara knew Ruby and knew her mother had friends in town, so she thought she might be overbearing with regard to her mother's well-being. She let the situation go and could only hope that her mother was sincere and not holding back any ill feelings toward her blooming relationship with a very wealthy and powerful corporate businessman.

"Money isn't everything," Norma said that evening as they looked over the orange hue of a horizon setting over the mountain.

"No." Clara was content being within the lushness of the forest around them.

"I hope you like him for more reasons than money is all I'm saying."

"I do. He's extremely smart, and he bought a bank, says I can manage it as CEO."

"Why you?"

"Why not me?"

"He could have any woman in the world. Why you?"

"He likes my passion and my creativity." Her eyes fluttered.

"You have great qualities. I don't mean that."

"What do you mean?"

"I don't know."

"You don't like that he has taken me away, do you?"

"You're a grown woman. I just don't want you to give up your passion."

"I won't give up my art if that's what you're afraid of."

"I'm not afraid. I just want you to always be you."

"I will, Mom. I won't let money change me."

She embraced her mother and, in that moment, a bald eagle soared above and Clara thought she saw some relief in her mother's eyes.

"You're the last generation right now, but I might be alive to see the fifth so I think about that too."

"Maybe this one will change our luck, Mom."

"Perhaps." Her beautiful smile was magnified by her hair blowing in the breeze.

They went to their art after a while and began to paint again together in that quaint little family cabin, and Clara waited for Quinton to call so she could confide that her mother has finally given her blessing.

"But she said she won't go to New York," she explained from the phone she had to take to a mountain peak in order to get reception.

She explained the Parkinson's to Quinton.

He didn't know what to say. "My mother received the print today. The original can go back."

Clara knew he was only doing what he knew best.

"Mom will like having that painting back at the cabin." Her voice was soft.

Three weeks later, the bungalow in West Virginia was sold and Clara helped her mother sell and donate the furnishings. They donated a sofa to the Salvation Army and an antique lamp to a thrift store. Norma kept a simple home, and even before minimalism was a thing she already had the concept down; Clara felt her mother was ahead of her time.

The wheelchair was still used since Norma grew to have pain in her back and legs attributed to aging joints, but her hands still painted with the most beautiful brushstroke. They received Helen's painting of a red rose magnified and had it packaged to be sent to the cabin. Clara wasn't going to the cabin, and although Norma had pain throughout her joints she still liked to drive. "I can still walk, you know," she said to remind her daughter how capable she was to be in the cabin without her able daughter. The cabin was too small for much more than their art, which they placed in the loft above, so they had ample storage space for something important. Clara put the wheelchair in the trunk and Norma set off to live in Vermont while Clara was left to wonder if she should be going to New York after all.

But things settled when Clara moved to New York and began taking weekend trips to the cabin. Quinton met her at their favorite shop where they ordered everything bagels and hot coffee. Clara was vegan and liked her bagel with hummus and veggies. Quinton liked to eat sausage, eggs, and cheese on his bagel. He enjoyed meals, and together they often liked to visit Ashley and Vinny; for being brothers they never tired of one another. The weather was changing as they neared October, and Central Park was becoming beautifully adorned in hues of orange and red. He had a surprise waiting for Clara in the back seat of a glossy black BMW, and when she peered into the back seat she found a crate and inside the crate was a fluffy puppy with a bow around her neck. "You got me a puppy?" She was in awe over the fluff ball.

"It's a surprise, of course."

"Thank you." She kissed him.

The puppy was an eight-week-old Pomeranian female she named Bella, and her fur was a pretty shade of red.

"You should name her Stella," Quinton thought.

"No. I like Bella." And the puppy gave her a lick on the nose.

Clara and Norma had a dog, a black lab, years before but Norma decided she could only support her daughter, and their dog was taken in by a friend. She was thirteen. Having a dog made her happy.

"So Bella will be going to the cabin in my place," he joked.

"No hard feelings," she said.

"None at all."

But it was true and they both knew it; Bella was company for Clara while she drove to Vermont for weekend trips; but the occasional weekend trips would become weekly trips as Norma's health declined. Clara had that inkling of a notion well beforehand that her mother's decline in health was going to progress beyond aching joints. Her mother did walk. But at a slow pace. There was a lot of walking in New York City, and Clara thought about having to care for her mother in those conditions.

She had Bella to take for walks around Central Park and a small balcony where she used puppy pads for Bella to do her business.

They were comfortable and Bella helped ease Clara's mind regarding her mother's condition.

"Thank God for cellphones," she told Quinton at the home bar where he was serving vegan-inspired eggplant Parmesan.

"Where did you learn to cook?" she asked, as he pulled the dish from the oven.

"Twenty-minute shows." He shrugged.

Quinton liked independence so it didn't surprise Clara that he would learn how to cook his own meals. The eggplant Parmesan turned out delicious and Clara enjoyed it with the Bruschetta he made as an appetizer.

"Did you get to FaceTime today?" he asked her.

"We did," Clara answered. "She went into town."

Norma continued to keep her distance from Quinton. She just didn't have the energy for it, she would say. Clara knew they couldn't be a normal family; she wasn't raised in the most normal sense. Painting was Clara's outlet and she was good at it. She painted with the energy and zest of the wild teen she once had been. Sometimes her art took on a dark sense, which she acquitted with being of an unusual type. While other girls did their nails and danced in fancy dresses, she would write poetry and sketch her take on a classic Dali piece of art. Her sense of time was never linear, and she painted glass melting above a flame and draining in a well that became lost time. She was eccentric. Plain but eccentric. She liked black licorice that she would moisten with her tongue and smother with sugar. In her art, the licorice would be ties that bound her lover's wrists.

"Why so dark?" she heard her mother's voice ask.

"Because this is how he wants me," was her honest answer.

Norma paid no mind to the art and tended her peonies while Clara designed silhouettes of phantoms biting an apple. She felt that food had a dangerous quality like most cravings do.

Her art, though, she contained away from Quinton who probably would not understand her.

Chapter Five

Quinton proposed to Clara over dinner in an elegant restaurant that had large windows overlooking the New York Harbor. He presented her with a diamond ring that shined like the lighting against the crystal glass they used to drink ice water.

Like water and ice, she thought. The combination of the two were sexy to her. Her mind wandered momentarily and when it came back to reality she answered with a hearty yes. He embraced her. They kissed and ordered dessert; she ate the cherry off the cheesecake. The succulent little fruit was like tasting heaven. Her senses indulged.

"My mother has been diagnosed with Parkinson's disease," she told her fiancé.

"I know, Mag-Pie," he said. "You already told me."

Mag-Pie. That cute little name only he ascribed to her.

"Oh," she said flatly.

"Are you feeling okay? You've been acting different lately."

"Yes. Sure."

"You'd let me know if there was anything?"

"I would," she stopped him, and held his hand.

She surrendered into her urges. She was getting married; the feelings, though, pulsated through her body and he felt it. There was a faint pulsating kind of energy between them like a benign electrical shock.

"What was that?" He looked at her.

"Love," she said, and he smiled huge.

The weather was cool, and Clara thought for a moment about kids. She was still young, going on twenty-three, and he was nine years older—exactly like her father and mother. How are such things possible? Clara and Quinton went home to Bella; she was good enough for a while, and Clara felt content having her mind off the having kids issue. The two of them parked themselves on the couch and Bella nestled between them. They were a family—a functional family—at least it seemed, and Clara was onto something she didn't really experience before.

Was she in love?

Was Quinton looking for love amid too many pick-pockets?

He wanted her. She liked that.

Sex was casual. He was a bottom. She didn't mind being on top, but she had a deep sense of yearning for something more—something larger than life—and that scared her. She wanted the passion fruit between them, but the sex felt contrived. She wondered if that was all there was to sex—the whole bottom and top—and persistence in the same way. She had Fernando, previously. She was a bottom. Quinton felt good, but the intensity was missing. She wanted a spark. The electricity was absent in the moment.

The man had proposed to her, given her a job and a kick-butt apartment in New York City overlooking Central Park—and she knew that asking for fire was asking for too much. She did her thing on top. He got off. It was good. She accepted it. Then they lay in bed—he was always one to fall asleep first—and she lay awake with the sounds of the city out the window. *The city that never sleeps,* she muffled under her breath. She rolled over and saw a bird out her window. She thought about her mother and how, in the morning, she would pack her bag and take a trip—her and Bella on the road. She wanted the fresh air offered by the country and she wanted to see her mom. "Moms are important," Clara told Quinton the next morning.

"Have a great time." He pecked her cheek and moved swiftly through the door. He was a man of business. Very formal. All things appeared legit on the outside.

Then she was in Vermont and everything was beautiful. Plentiful. Sexy. The trees were so lavish she felt momentarily like a body would feel rubbed in hot oil. She thought about penetration. She thought about something—she didn't know what—being the spark of interest. And Norma stepped outside.

"I didn't know my beautiful daughter would be here."

They embraced.

The hugs lately felt good to her. She had her mom. A man. A dog. Life was good.

"I just got here," she said, and they rocked in the porch swing. Bella came up the stairs after doing her business.

"What's that cute little bugger doing here?" Norma was smitten. The dog was precious.

"She's Bella. Quinton got her for me."

"What's that on your finger?" Norma didn't miss a beat.

"He proposed."

"With a rock the size of Texas."

Norma looked like she wanted to light a smoke and chat about horse racing. At least that's the image Clara had of her mother momentarily like a flashback of an earlier memory. She was certain they'd had that kind of conversation before.

"How did you find a man who'd buy you a dog and a ring?"

"And the apartment. The bank."

"Are you losing your independence?"

"Not at all."

"I'm sorry to say this my daughter, but the clear definition of all you described is dependency."

"No. I could always leave."

"How?"

"In my car."

Norma laughed.

"Well, he sure doesn't own the car, does he?"

"Not at all."

"The dog?"

"She's mine."

"You share'n her?"

"He likes Bella..."

"But?"

"He's not home much."

"No wonder you came to see me."

"Don't say that."

When they went inside, Clara was delighted to see her mother's fresh paintings displayed about the room on easels; there were impressionistic blends of peonies and her mother created accents of light just like Helen used to paint.

"Why don't you give my portrait a go?"

Clara excelled doing portraits. Her paintings were often of faces behind masks or silhouettes because she feared the details of perfecting the lines in drawing a human face when she began drawing in high school.

"Remember how bad I used to be?"

"You did a gorilla."

Clara laughed.

Her mother was right. And Clara painted her a portrait. Norma saw beauty in herself she hadn't felt for a long time. The absence of lines in her face reminded her of her youth when her body didn't hurt.

"They think it's arthritis," she told Clara.

"Before the Parkinson's?"

"Yeah. Before."

Norma wasn't well. Clara knew it was only a matter of time, and she watched as her mother aged, but her diagnoses were disconcerting ever more. She put the thought aside and asked, "Do you think I'll ever be as good as you and Grandma?"

"Even better, kiddo." She nudged her daughter's chin, and they turned away from art for the evening. Norma made a fresh salad with avocado, which Clara loved. She had a passion for things that delighted her senses. The school officials thought she was on the spectrum, but Norma wouldn't hear any of it. She refused. Her daughter was a prodigy in her eyes, and after high school she signed her up for a two-year private art school. Clara couldn't overcome her fear of doing portraits, so that evening she broke ground with Clara. She knew her daughter would continue to reach milestones. She was always progressing. They ate by a gas burning fireplace Norma had inserted before she moved in—at a small table for two in a cabin seemingly made for two.

The Parkinson's began with tremors in her left foot, jaw, and face after the arthritis in her joints that occasionally had her in the wheelchair. Norma had left her life at the stables and teaching at the school in West Virginia. Years earlier, she had begun there as a sub, advanced to an assistant teacher, and graduated as a lead teacher for the four-year-olds. She worked the stables on weekends. Clara knew what a sacrifice her mother did to work two jobs while helping her daughter through art school. Clara felt as though she owed her mother her life.

Then the tremors progressed to shaking in her hands; the brush was hard to hold, and Norma stressed that she could not paint. Clara brushed her hair and held Norma's hand gently to apply the paint. In the moment, their bodies became one: The lightest touch of Clara's hand helped Norma stroke the canvas with acrylic. As the disease progressed and riddled her hands, she decided to use more oils and pastels where impressionist touches to the canvas gave Van Gogh a run for his money.

Clara used oil on canvas as an impressionist design could complement her mother's works as they both created worlds that were whimsical and fantastic. Norma designed fireflies among the stars as Clara added dark blues, and hues of intense black and navy made fields of evergreens more dramatic.

And Quinton called. Her service worked.

"They put up a tower," Norma marveled. "He can call you now."

Bella barked as Quinton's voice echoed from the speaker.

"Would love to see you darlin'." He beamed from the smartphone.

Clara wouldn't put herself on FaceTime. She loathed the unshaken way she looked with unkempt hair. Quinton didn't care. He relished the way she looked at him with those field-of-evergreen eyes. Clara looked to Norma whose posture became somewhat awkwardly bent when she tried to sit. Her hands and joints were riddled with pain and Clara could see the tension in her eyes. She felt that perhaps Quinton needed to see the point-of-view of Norma, but they were nestled in the cabin for two.

"We plan to see Ruby today," Clara told Quinton.

"That's great," he said back, trying to be cool because really he wanted her back. But he understood.

"But tell me again, who is Ruby?"

Clara laughed. "I haven't really told you about her yet." She had a whimsical way about her in the face of adversity. She batted her eyes and thought her mother must be thinking how much she didn't care for a man much unless he looked like Elvis.

54

But Norma was situated comfortably despite her feeble body, and she was dead asleep with her head rested on the chair.

"Oh. I thought I might have forgot," he said with a kind of charm that made her think … if only he could sing. But he couldn't. He couldn't hum a note, and that part died with Elvis.

"Ruby lives in town. Mom really dotes on her."

"Then she must be an artist." He felt like he really understood Norma.

"She's an artist in the garden."

"Does she dabble in paint?"

"No. Only Mom does that."

"Well, I could really use some help at the bank."

Mercantiles & Trustees struck Clara as a kind of oxymoron and she laughed subtly when she saw its large golden logo glaring brightly among the city's brick and mortar … or skyscrapers and glass. The city was much different from the rolling West Virginia mountains, and the bank was grand. Much larger than her experiences, but she excelled in all things banking despite having gone to an art school. Banking paid her bills, and art kept her sane. In three years, she worked her way from teller to mortgage loans processor. Now she was overseeing the whole operation, going into her fourth year. She would have been overwhelmed had she not had Norma for a mother. What paid the bills now pays Norma's medical expenses. She had a salary of over four hundred thousand dollars a year as Quinton's branch manager.

"I have to help Mom" is all she could say.

"You have the Internet. Can you do some work from home?"

Clara huffed momentarily, but her mother slept and she wasn't tied up at the moment.

"I'm currently not doing anything."

"Then you can finalize that lending plan?"

They were corporate. Quinton had a large-scale toy store factory lending pending and he wanted the deal on the books.

"I can do it," she said and opened her laptop.

She was smooth talking numbers and finance with city officials. Nothing bothered Clara. She was elegant, poised, and sharp. Quinton doted on her. She looked like an hour-glass frame with a petite neck upon her shoulders, and he loved to escort her to the dinner parties.

Their first dinner out was with Vinny and Ashley, and they cozied up at *Lounge Fly* on Boulevard West where the toy factory owner, Sir Maverick, as they referred to him, though he was Maverick Square to most, saw Quinton and decided to talk business. Clara was introduced as his apprentice, as he winked, and she shook hands with the going-to-be first-time trillion-dollar man who also owned Maverick Saint Square: an entire city block that housed Maverick Saint Toys that were well stocked with the latest in all media. His refineries in Texas made his name appear in the catalogues of wealthiest across the nation.

Clara sat down and together Quinton and Clara banked capital on becoming Mr. Square's personal lender. The dinner was the month prior and while at the cabin she processed his lending on the slowest Internet connection possible. *So much for new towers,* she thought, but as the call ended and all things were final, Clara could happily push send and sign off—and five hours later they were off to see Ruby.

56

Chapter Six

"He proposed." Norma darted a finger to Clara. The umbrella she used to balance herself tossed to the side, she gave her hair a wring and parked herself at the table.

"Hello to you too." Ruby winked.

"Sorry that Mom can just let herself in." Clara winced.

"That's the only way to come inside from the rain," Ruby bellowed and shook the umbrella over the sink and laid it in a basin. "The rain just started," she said and began the coffee kettle. Then she retrieved the mugs from the cupboard.

Ruby's abode was quaint for two like the cabin. She had hardwood floors the color of maple syrup and heavy burgundy drapes. Ruby had red hair since the day she was born, hence the name, and she turned in her chair to find Bella snooping in the compost.

"What's this?" Her lip quivered when she talked. She blamed the damn meds.

"She's Bella." Clara chuckled. "I hope you don't mind her coming in from the rain."

"Do I have a choice?" Ruby cackled and slapped her leg.

"Mom said you liked dogs."

"I love animals," she hollered, and the rain poured heavy over the tin roof.

"Do you have any?" Clara wanted to be friendly.

"I have the chickens and the horses."

57

"You haven't had the horses since high school, darling." Norma was frank.

"I have them in my mind and soul." She was equally candid, and the kettle whistled.

"Still serving that instant stuff?" Norma looked to the kitchen.

"You hear the whistle blow'n! Means I'm using the instant stuff."

"Still no percolator?"

"Would I be using the tea kettle if there was something percolate'n?"

"Sorry I asked," Norma huffed.

"I'm sorry dear." Ruby shuffled her feet with a cup of hot coffee filled to the brim. "Norma says something about a proposal?"

"Yes…" She sipped her coffee.

"I hope you like it black and dark. I don't have a stash of cream or sugar to lighten it up."

"Dark roast straight up." Clara chuckled again.

"Let me get a look at it."

"Don't need to," Norma perked up, "you can see the thing from China."

"Men don't serve much good, do they?" Ruby had a past. She kept it clean.

"He's been good to me."

58

"How old is he?"

"Thirty-one. Almost thirty-two."

"That's what's wrong with him."

"His age?"

"He's too damn old." Ruby was prying.

"Mature." Clara was astute.

"No? Well then, I should say you're too young."

"I've always looked much older."

"You're twenty-two, missy."

"How old were we?" Norma chimed in.

"Too young also. And dumb," Ruby snorted.

"I think I'm making the right choice."

Clara didn't have a second before Ruby piped in again. "What choice you talking about?"

"The choice to marry him."

"Shouldn't marry. Not ever. Not a man."

Clara couldn't resist. "As opposed to marrying a woman?"

Ruby shrugged. "Sure, why not?"

Norma laughed. "We sure should have!"

"Would have been better off!" Ruby bellowed like a loud guffaw and spilled coffee down her blouse."

"Now I've done it."

"It wipes off," Norma said.

"Not all scars do dear." Ruby turned to Clara, almost a tear in her eye.

"He's not going to hurt me." Clara felt sincere.

"They all say that dear."

Ruby took off her shirt to reveal a soft, plush pink tank top beneath her blouse.

"You both look so beautiful." Clara couldn't resist.

And they did. For two women at sixty, they were wrinkle free and flawless in Clara's eyes. They shined. The years of abuse couldn't touch them then. Couldn't age them.

"And so are you doll." Ruby was sweet.

They drank their coffee. Bella sniffed in the corners.

"What brings you over today?" She smiled.

"Coffee…" Norma raised her cup.

"Oh?"

"Yes. It's empty." She grinned.

"I'd tell you you know where the pot is if those legs of yours weren't getting loose."

"Never say such things," Norma cackled lightly.

Clara giggled.

Before moving to Vermont, Ruby worked the West Virginia stables with Norma. They were sisters from other mothers—best friends since high school.

Vermont was their place outside West Virginia. They used to frequent the cabin together as kids when Helen would take them away to paint. Ruby bought the small log cabin not far from them when she left her husband, twenty years prior.

The cabins were a refuge for abused and battered women.

Clara wondered then if she too would seek solace in the cabin away from men; the cabin wasn't for them, and the women in her life seemed to have a similar kind of demise with men in their past. Clara could appreciate the history of the place; the cabin was meant for women who took their daughters to paint.

Clara put on her parka and entered the outdoors. The rain had stopped and the ground was piled with leaf litter. October turned to November and the women talked together on the weekends. Especially the weekends Clara stopped by to pay them a visit. She loved to travel with Bella who looked dashing in a yellow harness accented with a daisy flower. In December, Clara exchanged that flower for a red collar that played "Jingle Bells." The bell accents were charming for the season.

Norma decorated lightly with a front door rug, small artificial Christmas tree, some garland, and a candle. The atmosphere was ambient and smelled of pine. *You come'n over before Christmas,* she texted her daughter who was in New York securing accounts for bankers. Quinton decided to join forces with an upstate bank to take his location outside the city. Buffalo was populated and he knew a good deal when he saw one. He continued to prosper in banking, gambled, lost on occasion, and invested in Wall Street. He had Clara who was liked by his family and appeared no younger than him. The age difference just couldn't be seen superficially. She had respect as the lead corporate loan consultant, and sales were natural for her. She looked exquisite in red lipstick and dazzled wearing her long, stretch silver earrings that hung like icicles from her delicate ears. She was happy.

Coming tomorrow, Mom, Clara sent back. She hadn't seen Norma's decorating.

Clara decorated her home in red and gold. The lights on the Christmas tree were classic white and she hung the lights over the banister. The grand entrance was accented with glass ornaments from a white tree. She loved having two trees. She wanted her mother to see her home. She hoped Norma would allow herself to be stolen away for a while.

Clara planned to tell her that they needed to paint the city. The surroundings of Vermont offered so much, so Clara wanted to broaden the horizon with something other than a vertical landscape but the city couldn't provide that much. She then wanted to bribe her mother using the second annual art gallery event coming in June, and although months away, she would have her mother at her wedding. She was determined to have her mother at her home at least once. The cabin offered refuge, but the city added color to her paint amid the gray. The city was art deco and chic, and she wanted her mother to enjoy a visit.

I am your daughter, she texted, knowing Norma would catch on that Clara wanted her there.

The New York City art gala was to feature nonbinary and/or underrepresented talents at its second annual art show. Clara felt it was a perfect way for Thomas and Paul to encourage community and strengthen the bonds of other same-sex partners.

Can you be here? Clara was anxious.

Can we first get through Christmas? Norma knew how to avoid the topic. It was true she liked having Clara at the cabin. Clara wanted some more of a normal family life, but she didn't exactly get to grow up normal. She still had friends from the friendly neighborhood of West Virginia, but her repertoire was growing in New York.

She wanted to tell Norma about Maverick Saint Square—an entire city block comprised of the lavish toy store in New York. The place was originally intended to be a factory that ended up gutted and turned into the hub of Christmas. Thousands of tourists flocked to the Big Apple to shop the toy store every year and Clara wanted to take her mother there.

Speaking of Christmas … Clara commented.

What about it my daughter?

The biggest toy store in all of the US!

Got it.

Clara huffed. Her mother was stubborn, but she was determined to bring her mother back from her next visit.

She was on her way when she got a flat tire. She pulled off the street and behind her a shiny Silver SUV pulled up behind her. A man opened his driver side door and approached her.

"It's a chilly evening for a flat." He was charming and wore work boots.

"I'm cold and even worse I've never changed a tire before."

"Well I have some tools in the trunk and I could take a look for ya."

"That would make the situation look a little brighter. Thanks."

"No problem. Let me get the jack and the wrench."

"I appreciate it!"

He brought the tools from the Range Rover and jacked up her vehicle. Then retrieved the spare from the compartment and tightened each bolt to ensure sturdiness and safety.

She smiled. His dog woke up and barked from the vehicle, and they shook hands. Clara grabbed for her purse to pay him, but he wouldn't take her money.

"You have a safe trip." He tipped his hat and climbed in. The engine roared and he waved goodbye.

She watched him disappear into the horizon.

"See, Mom," she spoke aloud, "not all men are bad."

"Shit." She came through the door. "Mom, that damn door is heavy." She heaved her luggage inside. "And I forgot to get his name."

"Whose name? And how long you stay'n? You packed enough for the both of ya, whoever he is." Norma was still sharp-witted, even if she was slower on her feet.

"The guy who changed my tire."

"You got a flat tire?"

64

"Yes, Mom."

"Well, he was good for something." She sniggered.

The Murphy bed was still down from the wall.

"You can have the bed. I have the La-Z Boy."

"Why are you in the chair?"

"My body isn't what it used to be."

"You're only sixty."

"Don't remind me."

Norma was the same woman mentally and emotionally Clara had always known. The Parkinson's was taking her body after the arthritis in her hands and knees made her body ache. The years in the stables were to blame. Norma worked her wrists guiding those horses, cleaning their feet, and tending the stables—and being on her feet during those twelve-hour days affected her knees. Then the Parkinson's. And Clara could half forget because in her mind her mother would live forever.

That evening they put on their favorite movie. They warmed popcorn over the gas range and Norma started a fire in the pellet stove: one of Norma's upgrades.

"The cabin looks beautiful, Mom." Clara took a glass of wine from her mother.

They sipped lightly and watched the psychological thriller that made them wince.

"Something about *Sleeping with the Enemy* gets me every time," Norma huffed. "I could just take ahold of him."

Norma collected every film the lead actress had out, and she watched them like a toddler did with the same book. Same story every time."

"The men in these movies are assholes, Mom."

"That's because all of them are."

Clara could roll her eyes, but she refrained.

"Mom, I want you to see my home in New York."

"A home? You mean skyscraper? Isn't it all glass?"

"It has a terrace. Overlooks Central Park. Mom, you'll still get to see trees. You should come on out.

"Ruby is coming by shortly." She changed the subject but Clara knew she was considering.

"This late?"

"I invited her for movie night."

"And beer?"

"Ruby only does a little gin and tonic now."

"That's your kind of woman."

"It is I suppose."

"You been friends a long time."

"She's going to outlive me."

"Don't say that, Mom."

"We both worked those stables. Wonder why she's still so active."

It was Clara's turn to change the subject, so she got up to look out the window when she noticed an ash tray.

"Mom, have you been smoking?"

"What are you looking for outside the window?"

"Ruby!"

"I forgot to turn on the porch light."

Clara shuffled her feet toward the door and flicked the light on.

"Are you still smoking, Mom?" She had a stern gaze upon her mother.

"Still? What do you mean? I quit over a year ago."

"Why the ashtray?"

"It's an antique."

"Why keep it?"

"Why else?"

"What do you mean?"

"I just said it's an antique!"

Clara left it alone after that.

And when Ruby showed, she was sporting another parka during an evening of cool rain... and the next week there was frost on the windows.

Chapter Seven

Central Park was a blanket of white. Quinton took to the television to put on Norma's favorite show. Clara was upbeat since her mother agreed to return home with her. Norma felt she did it to make certain her daughter arrived home safe, because certainly no man could be trusted, and that tire didn't look right. Norma grabbed her pastels and took to the city. She wanted a canvas on the balcony and she intended to capture the green that was housed in that city, and she wrapped her body in a warming blanket and watched her breath turn to frost. Quinton joined her outdoors as he said, "Merry Christmas, Mom." Norma didn't know how to act; he wasn't beating them, and he was always dressed so sharp.

"You are blocking the light," she said as he saw his shadow looming across her canvas. He stepped aside.

"Sorry about that, Norma."

"No need to be sorry."

Norma continued to paint Central Park before she asked him, "You smoke cigars?"

"No, I don't," he said flatly.

"You smoke any of that funny stuff?"

"What are you getting at … if you're trying to find something wrong with me…"

She waved. Brushed him off and applied white to the evergreen.

"Mom," Clara said from the glass doors, "it's time for Christmas dinner."

"I guess my paint will have to wait." She winked.

Quinton held out his hand to escort her inside. She planted herself at the head of the table. Quinton looked perplexed initially but assisted her with scooting her chair closer to the table. Clara had made a ham for her guests: Athena brought a friend. Vinny and Ashley moved in closer. Clara didn't eat meat, but she knew the men would prefer some carnage upon the table. She smiled as Quinton took another chair, his usual seat being occupied by Norma of course, and Bella sat at his feet. Athena's date, or friend, was a sharp bachelor who owned another hotel chain that spanned coast to coast and brought unfathomable revenue.

"Last year's financial disclosure doesn't lie," Athena marveled inconspicuously within the kitchen as Clara salted the potatoes.

Ashley eyed Vinny who gave a nod in the affirmative. "An island, Mom. Three hundred and fifty million dollars." Vinny also raised his glass.

"So, Mom," Quinton said to Athena, as he tore a steak knife into the honey glazed ham belly. "Does your friend like ham?"

"I don't know," she huffed. "Why don't you ask him."

"Enoch, is it?"

"My mother was Catholic," he said in explanation of refusing the ham. "I'm sorry, I don't eat swine." He wasn't tender.

He had slick black hair and a thin neck. Clara imagined pointed shoulders and protruding bones beneath the blazer.

"What club is the jacket?" Quinton ate the swine.

"The yacht club," he professed and swiveled collard greens into a dinner fork.

"Enoch, are you also a member of the polo club?" Vinny wasn't eating much of anything. Ashley placed her hand on his thigh. "As a matter of fact, I am." He returned his gaze with a glint in his eye from the above chandelier.

"And how about golf?" Ashley was sweet. She ate everything.

"Not so much." He thought for a moment. "I tinker around with it..."

"Tinker? With a golf club?" Quinton was edgy.

Athena gave him a long, cold stare.

"Kind of like the inside of an engine." Vinny snickered.

"No, I don't think so. What do you mean?" Enoch wasn't playing with them.

"Just an interesting word choice." Vinny raised his glass—an old habit for a long dead habit.

Enoch went back to the collard greens.

Clara, at the other end of the table, looked to her mother. "How's the painting coming along?"

"Paint? Are you an artist?" Enoch was inquisitive.

"They both are." Ashley beamed when she talked.

"What do you paint?"

"Anything really," Clara said.

"Do you have a favorite subject?"

"Flowers." Norma respectfully gave a one-word answer as she chewed delicately on the baked potato.

"A favorite medium?"

"Acrylic," Norma said beautifully.

"On canvas." Clara smiled.

"You like oils and pastels?"

"Oh yes." Clara loved to discuss art.

"Has anyone ever told you you look like Elvis?" Enoch asked, turning his attention to Quinton.

"Yes, Enoch. They have."

"Maybe you should paint him." Enoch was amused.

Athena wasn't easily amused or dissuaded.

"Tell them about your island." Athena turned to him.

"I'm taking the yacht there in the spring."

"He's asked me if I'd like to come along."

"The family can come along if you'd like." He looked modest enough.

Enoch was tall and thin. He and Athena were a perfect match with bodies of a runner, and he appeared equally athletic and even matched Athena's love of scarfs about the neck; however, he removed his satin scarf while eating. Athena loosened her pink wrap but appreciated having a cute appearance.

"An island and a yacht?" Ashley buttered her potatoes rather than slathering them in gravy.

Quinton appreciated Clara's cooking, especially since she served a dish for everyone, including those who were not vegan. She served fried red potatoes garnished with rosemary, and Enoch thought it was odd to serve more than one potato.

"Perhaps overly zealous," she said, "but not everyone likes the same thing." She wondering if it all was too much.

"I happen to like red potatoes." Enoch was smiling.

"So, who wants to sail away to a private island on a yacht?" Athena marveled and Quinton looked displeased.

Athena had one divorce on the books, and her recent departure from Vinny's father was news to the family. Clara wondered if Athena thought about either son who had to bear witness to her change of heart so readily.

"Mom," Vinny started, wiping a bit of gravy from his upper lip, "when did you leave Dad?"

It was obvious Athena was having an affair.

"Your father didn't tell you? It was last March."

"Why didn't you tell us?" Vinny was composed.

"I did tell you. You just weren't listening."

"When, Mom?"

"I told you your father was leaving."

"Leaving?" He was perplexed. "I thought you meant on a business trip."
"Well, that too. But no, he was leaving … we just grew apart, Vincent." She huffed. "We both weren't happy."

Athena found out her husband was having an affair, and she took off from work to vacation on the islands and so she explained he had the affair first. Athena did not accept his apology when he admitted to infidelity and decided to move on emotionally despite staying in the home together while she worked out their assets. She reasoned that her affair was acceptable. She didn't care that he wanted to reason with her to stay.

"I don't know why he told me in the first place." She sniggered and asked for a shot of vodka to chase with a lemon.

Athena liked to drink as much as she liked money. She was a wealthy and successful woman, and no affair was going to be acceptable. And in order to have the upper hand, she seized the heart of a man who could continue to provide.

"What island?" Vinny inquired further.

"It's among the Virgin Islands." Enoch was simple in his address.

Norma had her place at the head of the table in the fashion she could understand; the head of the table was proper in her own right. She didn't come from money, but she knew how to entertain and be entertained. Quite frankly, she was ready to retreat to her cabin in Vermont where life was simple—a place where her painting wouldn't be interrupted. But she respected her daughter, and Quinton seemed to truly love Clara. She let down her guard against the strong-headed Athena and thought her painting could be a thousand times as elegant as anything else money could buy. She also reasoned in her own mind that

Athena went through the trouble to produce prints of her work and sell her art for décor in a newly developed hotel chain—that hotel chain, The Regal Hotels was owned by Enoch, himself. Together they were all on the same page at wondering if Athena's side of the story was the total truth.

Vinny did not appear convinced, but he had only recently departed from his wild ways when Ashley was going to leave; his love for his wife was thick, and he knew he'd have to give up the bottle of tonic—something he figured Athena wouldn't do. He wondered if her love could penetrate the superficiality of fine wine, martinis on the side, and five-star hotels. Athena became an entrepreneur at the young age of twenty, and she knew how to close a business deal with lock and key; she was on fire and was damn good at dealing with extreme wealth. Vinny might have faltered under the pressure of being his mother's son and Ashley reasoned with that.

"Get help or get out," she cried at their table one night. She didn't mean it entirely but Vinny knew he couldn't lose his best thing. Hence, Vinny went to rehab for six months as an inpatient for alcohol addiction and abuse.

They all drank around him, and he stayed true to himself and his wife; he swore to Ashley that he'd never let her down.

"We have something to tell you, Mom." Vinny looked to his wife.

Ashley smiled.

Get help or get out. The words echoed from the past in his mind. Then, he understood why...

"We're going to have a baby." Ashley beamed.

Athena dropped her fork.

"Already?" she asked. "How? When you just got out of rehab?"

"I was already pregnant..." Ashley began.

"She had a miscarriage," Vinny explained.

"I'm sorry. I did not know." Athena wasn't complacent. She was truly sincere. Ashley was special and that she knew.

"She told me about the baby after the fact."

"What fact?"

"I told him he needed to stop drinking."

"The miscarriage happened while I was in rehab."

"Oh. That's terrible. I'm sorry to hear that." Quinton looked to his younger brother.

"She was alone." He touched his wife on the knee.

"But I'm not alone anymore." She kissed him.

"Congratulations." Athena tinged her glass with a dinner fork.

"That's for the rest of us..." Enoch raised his glass.

"Bottoms up!" Vinny raised a glass of sparkling water.

"To Ashley and Vinny," Clara toasted them.

"To us." He kissed her again.

Chapter Eight

Christmas Season was over, and Clara went to work at the bank where she met the famous Maverick Saint Square who was borrowing to open another store chain across the West Coast. He desired having a franchise among his many investments and Clara knew how to get him the best deal. She was sharp-witted regarding numbers and was expedient to learn lending and took her knowledge to investment deals. Quinton was excelling in making business arrangements and sub-contracted with the local builders to create a business chain in California. He partnered with Maverick to set up a hotel, bank, and store in place of an old mall that had been long outdated. The mall came down and Hotel Athena went in its place aside Maverick Saint Square—a lavish décor shop that housed not just seasonal gifts but focused on home interior decorating and remodeling. Quinton's know-how in real estate gave them the edge in providing a desirable product in a booming market. Clara oversaw the deals and made sure the finances went into the proper banking accounts. She was responsible for multi-billion-dollar corporations and her clientele was exceeding her limitations. She would need hired help who she could train, but first she had a wedding to plan, and that's where Norma stepped in.

"My only daughter getting married," Norma said as she walked with a long gait and needed the wheelchair more often than before. Her hands trembled and the paint was dried to her fingers.

Men have no place in our lives, she huffed to herself, as she gazed out the window and turned to Clara who was holding a *Bride's* magazine.

"Mom," she was delicate, "I was about to show you my dress."

Clara's life became too fancy. She was possibly deluded by all the hype they had in their lives. Norma just washed the paint brushes and turned with a smile.

"You're going to look fabulous, I know." She tried to entertain the idea of a man taking up residency in her daughter's life. Norma moved toward the model wearing a gown.

"She doesn't look half as good in it as you will."

And that was that. There was no viewing pictures or chatting away over delicacies or details. The dress was exquisite and Clara took the remark as her mother's best try at a blessing. She put the magazine in her designer purse and zipped it shut.

Clara picked up her paint brush and Norma looked pleased as though for a moment she had her daughter back, as if she ever lost her. She painted a starry kind of night in detail as if the naked eye could behold the cosmos in fine detail. There were constellations bursting forth in prisms of colors and intimate lovers on the threshold of madness as one tips the tequila and the other salts her naval.

"When did you become such a lush for such a landscape?" Norma saw the spice in her daughter's pizzazz.

"When I became your daughter." Clara dreamed among her mother's paintings of being one of the fine women she created with accuracy in a brush stroke.

"I didn't teach you that." Norma was curious.

"You did mother. Through art."

Norma never realized that what she had been painting all along was love over hate. Perhaps Norma did dream of it, too, but she lost the heart for it all. Her hidden desires were refined by paint as if the notion of romance was lost in those she created.

Clara was taking the art form to another level as she gave great detail to her subject's fingers that were like wax to touch because the lemon and the salt remained there as their embrace portrayed an almost fatal kind of attraction. As if love could not be so thick. In Clara and Norma's world, the deeply concentric dance they played around the topic of love was earnestly delivered in the medium of art. But for Clara there was more than hope and desire behind the quill. She wrote of love in her journals beginning at age seven when she thought a boy in school had a crush on her. She was later crushed when he moved away.

"Oh well, more fish in the sea," Norma had said and glided away into the night and left Clara alone to ride out the night in her woe but unable to comprehend then the great pains men had been in her mother's life. Norma only faired well because she had a daughter to raise. In that respect Clara saved Norma.

Norma took Clara away from men. In that way she saved Clara. Saving one another created a strong hold between the two, and Norma never dreamed of someone coming between them.

Clara knew she had as much a blessing from her mother that Norma could muster and so she returned home to New York City in the bustling heat of July where she would wed Quinton Newman at the grand Athena Hotel where two hundred guests would hither inside from the heat and Norma would stay in the shadow of the dining hall. Remotely happy and proud but always so very hesitant. And after the formal sermon in the after party hours, Quinton would ask his new mother-in-law for a dance as he offered to push her wheelchair to the center of the floor; as the guests gathered including an obviously pregnant Ashley, Norma didn't smile, nor did she frown, but she wondered while in plain view of her belly, if her daughter was going to be blessed with a baby and have a life she never knew. Norma was breaking.

Or more aptly Quinton was breaking the barrier Norma had put around her, and although her hands were trembling, she felt somewhat subdued by the idea of love.

"He's charming," Ruby said from the corner of the reception hall later that evening and Norma huffed. "He better be."

Ruby chuckled and the two were a pair who would never entirely break or sever the cord that Norma said would always bind them. Norma danced on her own two feet. She danced with Quinton and the feeling of a man in her arms was dangerous territory. She almost cried. But she held back and kept her head over his shoulder. She didn't need the wheelchair for that occasion but for the first time in ages she wanted a cigarette. She sniggered over the thought of it and decided she would paint a woman having a puff. The idea of painting a cigarette smoking banshee of a woman made her laugh. Quinton tightened his grip as her legs nearly folded from under her. She hadn't told her daughter, but she started a new medication for the arthritis in her hips and she wondered if the rest of her joints would begin to collapse—she wondered how long it would take before she couldn't lift a paint brush. She considered the banshee and the cigarette when the meaning of life became comprehensible—you do whatever the hell you want to do especially if no one else is getting hurt. *Eat the cake* was an expression that came to mind. Norma thanked Quinton for his generosity, and she moved briskly toward the cake; she could literally eat the cake as the occasion also seemed to call for it. She was more apt to forget the cake and watch her weight but what the hell good did it do? Her body was breaking. She was arthritic already and diagnosed with a disease that would cause her body to lose its capacity for dancing. So she ate the cake while thinking about dancing.

Her daughter's wedding reception was the last time she'd dance. That notion stuck in her mind; it was better for her daughter to see her dance than to remember her as the snooty mother-in-law who refused to eat the cake. *Just dance* was her new motto. Clara embraced her mother and they chatted and they mingled. The guests were happy. The heat index outside was blazing hot and when they got outside at the end of the day, Quinton had a limo waiting for his new wife and Norma knew they were to venture to Key Largo—a destination that was Clara's choice because the West Virginia in her wanted adventure. She was set to go deep sea diving and tour the only living barrier reef in the Continental U.S. Clara wanted crystal clear water and pristine sandy beaches. Quinton assured her she would find that at Key Largo. And he also knew Everglades National Park would help to hone the quality of *Wild and Wonderful* that West Virginia was known for.

"It's not the Caribbean but it will do," Athena told Norma as Clara and Quinton entered the limo and Norma waved them off once again feeling she could cry.

But Ruby beat her to it. "I remember her in diapers," she said and gave Norma a tissue. Norma was reluctant and turned to Athena who was already walking off because Norma wanted to refuse their incessant request to join them at his three-hundred-fifty-million-dollar island. They were of so much money Norma couldn't reason with it; all she had known was terrible relations with the opposite sex and immersing herself in art. Hence, she had left Virginia for Vermont and the old hunting cabin in the woods. As Ruby drove them home from New York, they sang along to Elvis.

"He's lucky he has that going for him," Ruby said from inside the old Chevy, and Norma laughed; they were on the same page.

"Took the words right out of my mouth," she hollered over the music.

In a way they were young again.

But the real young ones were knee deep in rich sandy beaches by the time Norma and Ruby made it home.

81

Clara had a margarita on the beach, and although this was the honeymoon phase of her existence, she thought about her mom. Norma was an angel to her, and she was blessed with a gifted, talented, and loyal mom who never had concern to have a man in her life. She couldn't help but wonder if she had let a man take her mother's place. Then she dismissed it. Mom had Ruby when her daughter couldn't be there. Clara had never dreamed of so much money and thought about how winning a trip to the big city to partake in an art show led to marrying a man who was akin to Elvis. His hair was turning a shade of silver, however, and Elvis never did turn gray. The weeklong beach trip filled her photo portfolio of ideas to paint later when she returned home. Clara felt the week was otherwise uneventful for Quinton but she enjoyed snorkeling, scuba diving, and touring the Everglades. Quinton tolerated it while she thrived on it. He did however get to dine in the fancy restaurants and enjoyed late night bands at the beach. His favorite spot was the tiki bar. Clara enjoyed a Pina Colada while Quinton was served an appetizer (lump of crab meat and other sea food) while she enjoyed a vegan burrito.

"We get to do this again," Quinton said between bites of scallops.

"Again?" Clara wasn't following.

"The yacht. Island. Remember?"

"Oh yes." Clara had a mouthful.

"You think we can get Norma to go?"

"Unlikely." She didn't want to leave her mom another week.

"Ask Ruby to come along."

She honestly hadn't considered that yet.

What she did consider was the differences between Norma and Athena, but what Athena did for her mother's art touched her deeply. She knew she wanted a relationship with her mother-in-law, but what she wanted more was for her beloved mother to see some good in a man that goes beyond Elvis, beyond whatever it was she saw behind the music. Or, perhaps, she thought, Norma needed to see more than the art, if only for her sake. Clara wondered if Quinton could paint or sing, if Norma would notice those qualities in him. Money didn't sway Norma the way art did. She thought then, too, what her own life would be like without art, and "incomplete" was the best term she had for the notion.

When they returned home, Clara had work to do for the banking business, and Maverick Saint Square was on her voicemail; he was doing a major re-set within his toy store and wondered if the loan could be processed to include a re-set for Texas—a completely new territory for any of his businesses. Clara returned his call to get yet another voice message system and she began to process the funds and found he had money tied up with Enoch in a plan to build real estate on the island; they were contracted to do renovations together. The connection was eerily close to home, and Clara could see their assets; Enoch was entirely a billionaire who gained wealth during ownership of sprawling corporations and had hefty stocks in the market. Athena was like a gem.

It was later, when Athena confided to Clara that Enoch wanted a professional to handle his assets, that Clara became overwhelmed. She was immersed in billions of dollars and was responsible for securing funds and assuring good investments. Her banking knowledge was pushed to the extreme, and although she wanted to tell Enoch that someone else would be good for the job, she succumbed to the pressure of being of assistance. Quinton then began asking her to venture with him on business trips; then it all came together—the private island getaway was a business proposition, and her clients were working together to join forces, so-to-speak, in development projects.

Quinton didn't have artistic abilities but he had brain power and that enticed Clara. She felt compelled to deliver because in that sense he aroused her nature. Being gifted smart was sultry and sexy. She confessed in the mirror the *Hound of Wall Street* aroused her senses. Her senses became keener with the development of her mother's demise. She was right; Norma had no interest in the private and secluded island.

"But it's like the cabin, Mom." Clara tried to reason with her.

"How so?"

"Seclusion."

"And how many people?"

"Mom, it's a private island worth three-hundred-fifty million."

"So?"

"So, you can paint something beautiful out there. Besides, you need a change in muse."

"My muse is in the woods."

"Your muse can be a tropical paradise."

"I like it here, my daughter."

"I do too. But go to the island. For me."

"I will do it all for you."

"Do you swear? You promise?"

"I promise," Norma huffed.

"Thank you, Mom." Clara hugged her mother.

She couldn't help but think that went easier than she thought it would.

Clara and her mother would FaceTime often. She loved to see her mother's face. Her latest painting. Her happiness.

Ruby went along too. They left in a yacht toward the tropical paradise Enoch then called Athena's.

Vinny wasn't amused but he went along with his pregnant wife.

"Better them than us." Quinton toasted Clara.

Quinton didn't want kids. Clara hadn't told Norma. They dined late over the balcony of a luxurious ship while Ruby and Norma chuckled in their private room.

"She never should have won that trip." Norma was morose in the moment.

"What disturbs you the most?"

"Years of abuse."

"I mean with her. Not you."

"Same answer."

"You know, I know very well where you're coming from."

"I know you do."

"Let Clara have a whole new experience."

"She is."

"Yes. Good. She is."

"I know."

"Let's turn in for the night."

Their room had two king beds. They slept softly beneath the covers. The ship was steady and they didn't notice the swaying or the breeze outside of the room.

Outside Quinton and Clara drank alcoholic beverages while gazing at the sunset and until past midnight.

They went to their exquisite room, and Clara felt a subtle change in her that night. With Quinton, her mother didn't need to be afraid. It was Clara who was afraid; time was passing them by, and she just didn't know if she needed to give Norma a grandbaby.

Chapter Nine

They sat beneath a canopy of soft beige linen and bamboo. Their rooms at the individual huts were simple yet elegant. There was simplicity that Norma didn't know came along with the rich. She was pleased. The men were down to business. Enoch laid out blueprints: Hotel Athena, a bank, a casino, a tiki bar, and boat access. He wasn't planning to let just anyone vacation there as prices to visit Athena's Island would cost upwards of nine hundred a night for the most basic room rate. The idea of such extravagance overwhelmed Clara if she thought about it too much. She took a deep breath and examined the idea that she accepted having things over giving Norma a baby to hold in her loving arms. Quinton interrupted her concentration with a hefty intrusion...

"I need you to run the numbers for the blueprints. If all costs are covered and we get a return on our investment, we will buy our own island." He chuckled.

Clara didn't feel they could afford an island exactly as their net worth wasn't quite Enoch's billions. The man had a yacht and a private jet. The island was a token really, and there they were with blueprints to build and monopolize. She smiled and left the room. She opened her laptop. She factored their numbers; she put every dime into a spreadsheet. What they would pay. What they would need in revenue. An outline of their profit margin. Hours into the work, she was tired. She hadn't seen Norma but found her in the natural hot spring aside Ruby. She stepped in up to her ankles and sat at the edge of the warmth as she turned her face to the sun.

"You look peaceful," Norma said.

"All this peace is going to be a bustling little place eventually."

"Just think of the now until then." Norma had a way of keeping her together.

The now was a hot spring. Tiki huts with soft linens. Straw roofs. Bamboo fixtures. It was Norma's aesthetic and Clara hated the idea of development in a place so beautiful. But with a stretch of the imagination, she conceded that perhaps they'd have their own island because it was the work of her husband who dreamed of turning their millions to billions. And just to think in her own mind—she would be a part of that.

Quinton didn't have a woman stealing his checks. But rather, tallying the assets for his business portfolio. Clara felt powerful in that. Norma felt something amiss came along with too much money. Like a bad taboo. Clara felt her mother watched too many bad movies. Ruby bridged the gap between them and would be ever present as the voice of reason.

"Maybe you should look within your soul to know truly who you are. And what you want," she said.

The truth was that Clara didn't know. She was just really good at math, and working the banking and dividends made sense to her.

Athena wrote her a brief text about next weekend's baby shower for Ashley. Clara didn't think it left much time to prepare. Ashley and Vinny decided to keep the sex of the baby a surprise, and so Clara wanted to do a soft palette theme for her gifts. The artist in her felt the baby needed honeycomb beige and hints of muted green.

Ashley gained an extra eighty pounds with her pregnancy and her size eight frame supported the adorable bump well. In the time that ensued, everyone became busy. They packed up and went home. Clara went shopping for the ensemble she hoped to put together. Norma went home to set up for art; she placed the painting of mangos in a fruit bowl over her kitchen window. The island did provide the muse Clara said she would be destined to find there. Ruby went home to cook and clean while Athena got busy with room décor; she was having her first grandbaby and she loved to decorate, a little bit to Ashley's dismay. Athena wanted her nose in everything while Ashley wanted to choose paint colors.

"How do you know what color to paint the walls when you don't know what you're having?" she huffed.

Ashley chose a soft gray with white accents. She was happy. Her baby shower came as a surprise to her, although she should have assumed. But Athena didn't say a word.

"It's a surprise." She beamed as Ashley was dropped off at Athena's by Vinny, who had promised to keep the occasion quiet.

Athena hoped for a gender reveal so she could host the surprise occasion for all their friends but settled on surprising Ashley anyway in the way she could. Ashley especially liked the diaper cake Mystique put together.

"I feel like I haven't seen you in forever." Ashley gave her a hug.

Her brother, James, wasn't invited. The shower was a party for the women, and the men decided to gather at Quinton's for a party in the man cave. The entire lower level was dedicated to having a display of collectibles; he especially liked hot cars. He didn't do NASCAR, but he loved a good Ferrari.

Ruby and Norma wouldn't be there. Norma felt the occasion was for Clara and her friends and didn't feel she knew Ashley that well. Clara felt Norma wouldn't let herself get to know anyone too well. But Clara showed at Athena's large, immaculate home in New Jersey—one of Athena's many estates. There they had a taco party and baby shower. Ashley loved authentic Latin food and the tacos were spicy ... being pregnant did not deter her from spice. Clara made enchiladas with everything vegan including the cheese, and Athena put together the bean dip and taquitos. Mystique brought fresh, homemade salsa and guacamole. Athena had Ashley's sorority sisters fly in from abroad and out-of-state, and she paid for everything.

James, Quinton, and Vinny talked over the bar, and Quinton gave Vinny a cigar. They smoked, ate any extra food, and watched the television that featured booze, women, and hot cars. They were men. The women got to be women. They were happy.

Norma was alone. She liked it that way in her cabin in the woods. But she fell, and no one was there to pick her up. She fell down the outdoor stairs and there was no one. Her back hurt. She didn't cry but lay there gazing at the perfect blue sky and hot sun. She got lucky, and a backpacker picked her up that day; he told her he had been past that cabin many times but he thought it was a deserted hunting cabin. He found her there lying on the steps.

"Can I get you some help?" He was earnest.

"Just pick me up and call my friend Ruby. She'll take it from here."

She was blunt and didn't think much of his being at the right place at the right time. He got her inside the house and she phoned Ruby.

"Thank you. She's on her way. You can leave now." Norma just didn't like men.

He left. She didn't get his name. And she never mentioned the incident to Clara who would only grow so concerned for her mother that Norma felt she would never leave her alone. And it wasn't that she wanted Clara to leave her alone, but she wanted to be alone. "It's one of life's many paradoxes," she often told Ruby.

Ruby would reason that she too wanted to be alone. They were a pair so introverted and withdrawn that their own family came to feel discontented in the distance they kept between them and others.

Clara had a sixth sense however, and she called her mother. "Mom are you all right?" she said into her cell phone.

"Why wouldn't I be all right?" Norma grew used to Clara's strange differences; one time in childhood Clara told her mother she saw a ghost. Another time, she was talking to seemingly no one. Norma accepted the ghost if she wasn't bothered by it, and she never was. Neither was Clara so the whole affair seemed harmless. Then there was the constant foresight exhibited by Clara that Norma couldn't find a reason for, such as when Clara told her mother, "Watch out," just before Norma knocked the toaster on her toe. "It's the evolution of human consciousness." Clara shrugged and walked away. Norma didn't have her daughter's gifts. As odd as the abilities were, Norma accepted her daughter's mysteriousness as exceptional qualities because maybe one day it would save her life. Clara shared a story from the hospital once when Clara had oral surgery at age five, about a patient who had dementia and was afraid the room was on fire. They blamed her *craziness,* but weeks later the room caught on fire from an electrical problem. *She knew,* Clara said to her mother, and *I saw her,* Clara confided.

"You saw who?" Norma wasn't convinced.

"The lady who always wore red shoes." Clara went back to playing.

Clara had always been strange or, if anything, abnormal, in that she strayed from the beaten path. That concept Norma could relate to: strange and beaten path. But she never wanted pity; Norma wanted a basic kind of life which meant she wanted to earn enough income to pay the bills and raise her daughter. In that she won. She had success as far as she was concerned. Clara thought so too. Clara wondered if her new affiliation with money made her mother feel any different about success and she certainly hoped her mother would not see her situation that way. Clara knew her mother was a success.

"Mom, you would tell me if something happened right?"

"Yes, I tell you everything." She didn't say it had to be right away.

"Okay, Mom."

"Go back to the shower," Norma spoke softly.

"I will. Okay. Are you sure something is not wrong?"

"I'm sure."

They ended the call and Clara went back to Ashley. Back to her thought, *it's better them than us.*

She had never considered if she wanted kids or not, but she knew she had ten years to figure it out: being twenty-three, she figured, she had that long to figure it out.

Ashley had the best two hours among friends and family. She ate the cake. She opened the gifts. They had lunch. Life was good.

Then Norma fell again. "This damn body acts like eighty," she said to Ruby who was helping her long-time friend to her feet.

Clara didn't figure she wanted to have kids and then she held Skyla; she was born in October and had red hair and blue eyes. She was seven pounds. Ashley was in labor twelve hours. Vinny saw his daughter and melted. Quinton wasn't into the whole situation. He saw her, he gave his bro a hug and he asked Clara about Maverick Square. She had nothing to say. She was in awe. Athena looked radiant for the occasion and she beamed.

"Red hair and blue eyes are recessive. Only makes up one percent of the population." She held her granddaughter and sat in the chair aside Ashley.

Quinton poked Clara again. "It's not time for business," she whispered.

"Let me know what's convenient for you." He stormed off.

She was perplexed and mostly just unfazed. She knew money could create a distraction in him. Or, perhaps, she should say business was a distraction. Money was just the result. Clara didn't quite know where she was in the affair of Maverick and his billion-dollar projects on the island. It seemed they were creating a mini *Wonderland* but ripe with casinos like Vegas.

"A mini Vegas then," her mother corrected her.

They were on FaceTime. Clara wanted to tell her of their new niece.

"She's got a set of great parents," Norma said.

"A set?"

"That would be two."

"Who else?"

"Grandmama and …"

"Enoch. And it's like you said Mom, Grandma."

"We'll see about that."

Clara ended the call. Right or not, Norma was and had always been opinionated. Clara's first boyfriend grew afraid of Norma. That really made her perturbed.

"Are you always going to drive them away?" a sixteen-year-old Clara asked her mother.

His name was Kelvin, and Norma saw a puny little guy that didn't add up. Clara saw a great soccer player and felt she came on too strong.

He blamed their breakup on the two of them going to separate colleges but Clara rolled her eyes. "That's in two years." She slammed her notebook shut and wondered who was going to have the backbone for Norma.

"All she said was 'Where's the rest of him?'" she explained to Ruby back in the day.

"Well she made him feel small. Boys don't like that."

"Yeah. Well. Whatever." A defiant but still charismatic Clara sniggered.

"Maybe keep the next one away." Ruby laughed.

Clara didn't date through college. She got the offer to show her art in a prestigious gallery in New York City and her life took off. Quinton was the next boyfriend and he was thirty-two. She was twenty-three. She felt bodacious enough having Quinton. She wondered what was missing.

"No one is perfect," *Counselor* Ruby said.

Ruby was usually their voice of reason. Clara confided in her just as often as Norma.

94

Quinton seemed to adore Norma; Clara figured he was so used to public attention with his stunning looks and was taken aback by a woman who didn't stop at his good looks and coveted charm. He was on a mission to win her over. Norma was scarred skin deep like penetrating the bone; men were a horror to her. Clara didn't have a father though and Quinton was filling that void in her life; she never knew a man could exist and stick around so long. He wasn't turning away. Not yet. Clara had a chance.

"She just doesn't like me," he confided in the kitchen.

"She adores you." Clara meant it.

"How the hell do you figure that?"

"It's not you she dislikes. It's the men of her life."

"The men of her life. Exactly."

"No, the men who were in her life. Not mine."

"They must have sucked real bad."

"They did."

Clara took a shot of espresso. "So you want more on Maverick Square?"

"Give it to me."

Enoch and Maverick were conspiring to light the island on fire.

"Casinos amid the lavish estate."

"I already knew that though."

"Hotel Athena will be the grand opening..."

"Casinos inside the hotel?"

"Yep."

"Anything else?"

"A full-on media room and theater."

"I wonder if that will spark any interest."

"The bank is getting calls to handle large investments. Investors are already invested. "

"I'm floored."

"You want to celebrate?"

"Yeah."

He wasn't wild but he settled a desire in her that night.

Norma never answered the phone. Ruby said she was okay. Just trying to grapple with the loss of her hands. Paint was the world to her. Clara wondered where her heart was in the moment. Norma was losing abilities in her hands. She seemed to be losing the ability to love. Clara grew in dire need of her mother to be well again and soon it would be a kind of relationship that went distant, somewhat dark, somewhat unrecognizable.

Norma wasn't herself. She grew in age and the distance became insurmountable. She became another person entirely the day she was diagnosed with dementia. Clara was losing her mother despite the fact she moved her mother into their home. Norma was spiteful.

"No ability in my hands," she grumbled.

With time her physical and mental health deteriorated and that would be how it was for nine long years. Long to Norma, but not enough time for Clara who would take her mother especially during the moments of lucidity.

"Who are you dear?" Norma was a kind and delicate woman after the dementia impaired her memories.

Clara showed her her art and Norma would return to her cognitively if only for a minute. She would also hang photos about her room.

But Norma would refute, "I prefer the art."

Clara was broken. She seemed to not have her mother's love even when Norma showed love.

"She doesn't know me most of the time." Clara shed tears to her husband who felt helpless.

"I can't bring her back for you but she's here now."

"She's here but gone." She rested her head on the table.

She went to Norma's room and found there the quiet. A resounding kind of peace flooded the room. Norma was cold.

Chapter Ten

Norma died ten years after Clara married Quinton, on the date of their anniversary. Her room was full of light, and full of art. There was a silence that coated Clara's senses. Norma died unable to recognize her daughter and had, the night before, recognized her own mother in a piece of art. Clara felt sadness and despair and tried with all her might to reason that her mother was with Helen and Lucille in Heaven, and together they were making art. She buried her mother at Hope's Paradise Memorial Park next to a gorgeous plot of land that was accented with a pond and a fountain. *Here rests a mother and a woman gifted in art;* her headstone had been ascribed to reflect the things Clara felt her mother loved most. Instead of celebrating her ten-year anniversary, she left their home and went to the cabin. There was only one painting that remained in that cabin, and it was the self portrait she painted herself; her mother was there in the spirit of a painting and gone in the flesh. *Bones in a box,* Clara thought of an old passage within a book. The thought of that grim prospect mortified her. She wanted her mother to be alive in that box and forget in her own mind of the morbid detail of decomposition. She wanted to flee the prospect of being in the world utterly alone. She could not give her mother the next generation; even if she had given her a grandbaby, Norma would not have remembered her. Norma's last days were eerily quiet and Clara grew morose knowing her mother would never return to her; she thought about how Norma lost art in the years of her Parkinson's Disease while movement in her hands was of a constant tremble rather than the fine motor ability required for a brushstroke.

"You could try abstract art, Mom," Clara told her.

"What's that?" Norma knew what it was, but she had no interest. Her art had always been accented in rich details and painted with lines.

Clara took out her easel and paint in that cabin. She began with hues of deep purple and toxic blue; not to convey the natural aging process but to show the diminishment of spirit.

Norma's art was in her daughter's home she shared with Quinton. In her home where her mother took her last breath in the moment Clara was not there. In the moment she was making her mother's waffles that she would complete with strawberry jam and chocolate syrup: a strange combination her mother asked for every morning. Clara blamed the dementia regarding her mother's changes. She had loved an old pair of hiking boots but later asked for red heels; there was a painting of a tango dancer in red heels. Norma's state of mind stayed attached to paint.
Clara wouldn't reason with the loss of her mother, and her husband remained within his business affairs.

Clara was set to go to the island on a trip with Enoch and Athena who were recently married around the time of Norma's death. Norma kept Clara at home most often; the timing seemed too perfect for her to have the opportunity to visit the bustling estate on Athena's Island and her grand hotel; the whole trip was complete with a yacht: *The Athena.* She was everywhere while Norma was gone. Clara didn't grow attached to Athena but she did accompany her husband's family on the yacht at Athena's Hotel on an island dutifully titled Athena's Isle. Athena was everywhere. They drank, they sang, they had kids; Ashley and Vinny had three children over the course of ten years with each of them five years apart. Clara still had Bella—that dog was her sidekick and had aged into blindness. She sat on Clara's lap as Clara observed the banter and posed the question: "How can you stand to watch them drink?" She didn't mind being obtuse in her condition.

Vinny drank sparkling water and winked. "I was the dumb shit," he said, "especially when I drank."

They didn't seem to handle the alcohol any better.

"Poor guy." Clara may have seemed distracted while in conversation with Vinny, but she heard Athena perfectly well, as her mother-in-law quickly turned her attention from Vinny to Clara.

"You had a hospice situation at home for so long. Must feel good to be here and away from everything else."

Clara learned much about Athena over the years and felt admonished to say, "Go to hell, Athena."

But she could only think it in her own mind. Vinny looked the other way as beautiful women passed by them. He then felt a sharp tap across his shoulder.

"Keep your eyes to yourself," Ashley said. "What else are you two doing over here?"

"Just shooting the shit." Vinny laughed. He had been caught looking.

He wrapped his arms around his beautiful wife and pulled her onto his lap.

"I only have eyes for you babe," he said.

"You better." She kissed him.

Clara wanted her cabin. But she loved Ashley and Vinny dearly.

She didn't go to the cabin that night. Her art became more abstract and she used that ability to conceal her disdain for that island. A place where most would relish in the delicacies and play the slot machines piss drunk. In that state she could side with

Norma who preferred the artistic expression of the quintessential vacation home she had with Quinton.

"Look who's here honey." Quinton entered the bedroom of their vacation abode.

"Hello." She sneered a grim smile.

Quinton was momentarily perplexed.

"Have I come at a bad time?" Maverick was a guest in their home as Quinton was the business partner he needed to create the banking clientele he sought after. Clara wondered if the relationship was a friendship at all and she thought how he only seemed to have business relations and other than Ashley and Vinny and seldomly James and Mystique, she didn't have a friend in the world; her life had revolved around Norma, and outside of mom was work. She then thought of Ruby who was alone at the age of seventy and still very capable. "Very capable," she let the words slip out.

"Who is, my love?" a graying Quinton said and Clara appeared closer to his age, or at least she thought so—felt so.

"Nothing." She didn't want to speak.

Clara stood from the bed. "It's good to see you, Maverick." She touched his shoulder.

"Likewise." He was monotone.

She stepped out on the sun-filled day and observed as Athena and Enoch drank at the Tiki Bar across the sandy shore.

Ashley and Vinny had their three children, Skyla, Raven, and River, who frolicked in the water. Mystique and James were invited and they stayed on the bow of the yacht overlooking the water. They had only one girl named Trinity because Mystique experienced life-threatening complications. At age five Trinity was close to Raven who was nearly the same age.

"Eleven next month, seven, and four," Quinton said.

Clara was very puzzled.

"I must have read your mind." Quinton forced a smile.

"What?" Clara was trying to understand.

"You're watching them so I thought you might be thinking…"

"Thinking what?"

"Why we never …"

"No. I wasn't thinking that."

"Do you ever think that?"

Clara recognized that Quinton was turning forty that year, and at thirty-two she really didn't feel concerned. Then the simple thought crossed her mind that over the course of ten years she didn't have a single scare. Not one. The thought bothered her momentarily only because Quinton inadvertently confessed he was thinking about the subject of not having had children. It perplexed Clara because she knew he had no interest and saw no reason for a change of heart.

"A precious heirloom," a voice said and Clara turned to find Athena.

"What?" She was perplexed once again.

"Oh," Athena huffed with the wave of her arm, half spilling the brandy, "you know how much I overhear things."

Athena, Clara reasoned.

It was always Athena. And certainly she'd been talking to Quinton.

"Don't let me sway you." She half smiled.

What else had Athena been saying? Clara's mind was chatty.

She decided to leave.

"Hope we didn't offend you," Quinton called out to her.

All she could think was that devotion meant nothing to someone like Athena.

James furnished Clara's Island Villa with photography he had taken over the years and as she looked at herself in those portraits aside Quinton she considered if she had wasted his time. With that thought she took a shower. Then she ate strawberries. Then she drew the curtains closed and slept through the night to leave the following morning.

It was her time in the cabin.

Ruby wasn't sweeping the front steps as she had been known to do while Norma declined. She knew her friend remembered her in spirit and although Clara would take her mother to see her, she wasn't aware anymore. In that Ruby lost her best friend long before she lost her best friend. Clara wondered if Ruby would visit and she intended to see her. She first wanted to paint but the canvases she liked to use were nowhere to be found. She considered that Norma hadn't wanted to entertain abstract painting and so she wanted to re-visit her mother's favorite styles. She opened the door to the closets and after some shuffling around she located a box of hidden, or seemingly hidden, acrylic and a canvas that was blank. When Clara picked it up she could feel the texture was off and she flipped it around to discover the work of a man on canvas. A man done in paint. *A man*, she thought to herself feeling extremely perplexed. She wondered if Ruby would have an idea of what this *man* was doing in her mother's beloved closet. A closet that stored all her hopes and dreams. Norma hated, or despised, men and Clara just couldn't grasp him being in *that* closet. Clara stepped outside with the portrait tucked beneath her parka. It was raining in Vermont that day. She didn't want her mother's work ruined. If that's what it was—but she could not fathom that anything else would be stored in that closet. She reached the front door and before she could knock Ruby opened the door.

"I heard you coming," she whispered.

"Heard me?"

"Shhh," Ruby whispered again.

Was Ruby losing her mind?

"Don't you mean you saw me?" Clara whispered along.

"No. You see, I have these new hearing aids. The damn things hurt my ears but earlier I could hear the birds better and I could hear you walking, cracking sticks with each footstep." Ruby smiled.

Clara felt relief.

"Here," she said, and sat in the chair, "let me turn them down." Fidgeting with the small ear bud made her hands tremble. Clara thought of Norma. She studied Ruby's hands and wondered how or when her mother had the dexterity to paint a portrait of such exquisite detail. She didn't waste any time.

"Do you know who this is?" She showed her the painting.

"I don't know who the hell that is... where did you find him?"

"In my mother's closet."

"Beats me."

"Are you sure you don't know..."

"I assure you I don't know."

Clara left it at that. They had coffee. Then that evening they had wine.

She hadn't heard from Quinton and wondered what was keeping him from calling regarding all his business propositions. She knew he wanted to work the Kensington client and he always called while she was away. That weekend he hadn't. She didn't bother him. He likely had too much to do.

Back at the cabin the rain had died down and Clara noticed the muddy prints on her front stairs. She hadn't ever seen someone near the cabin and wondered if there were hunters nearby, but the cabin was situated on a reserve and hunting on the premise would be illegal. She also wondered if she should be alarmed by the presence of muddy boot prints because she had always suspected she was alone. The thought of someone intruding or lurking near the cabin bothered her. She did understand too that the small cabin could look like a hunting cabin to anyone who was not familiar with the area. Then she also considered the Appalachian Trail that wasn't too far away, but still, they would be off the beaten path. The area was excellent for wildlife and photography so she shrugged it off and hoped for the best. Then Quinton called.

"Yes dear?" She was being cute.

"I'm home. When will you be?" He was kind of brief but she didn't mind.

"I'll be heading out today. You want me to take care of the Kensington file?"

"That would be great hun."

They hung up. It was like him to call about business. She considered that they were often referred to as the power couple. She picked up the portrait from the Murphy bed and returned it to her closet. She took one last look at Norma's face in the only painting, the only one she knew about, and spoke out loud, "Happy Mother's Day, Mom." She thought she would cry not having her mother on her second year without her.

Time was going by. She took one last look, too, at the closet door she shut, wondering who the hell her mom had painted.

Clara made it back to New York and left her car in the parking garage. She walked several blocks alongside Bella to the three-floor condo she shared with Quinton. That year they bought a larger home in New Jersey near Athena. Clara knew she wanted her eldest son to give them a grandbaby. Clara didn't know if they could conceive. They were too busy to care. Then Athena pried if they would begin consulting a doctor. Clara couldn't give Norma a grandbaby either. She wondered if Norma would have asked for one if the dementia hadn't been so cruel. If she could have remembered her. If only they had known one another more intimately because who the hell was the man in the portrait. How many secrets had Norma been harboring?

106

She entered the front door. There was no one around. The chef was out. The cleaners were gone. There was no nanny because they had no need for one. Ashley and Vinny had one. Her name was Susan. She was a doll. They doted on her ingenuity when caring for the children. Her brains, her expertise, her gifted nature made them relish every moment of having her with them. Clara thought then that perhaps she and Quinton were missing out. Skyla was getting so big. Raven and River were too. Mystique had Trinity and Clara was alone. Her mother was gone. She wanted to go into the bedroom to talk it over when she heard the bed. The clear indication of the headboard against the wall. It needed to be tightened. Quinton wasn't handy and fixing the damn thing wasn't important. They weren't exactly that sexually active. She blamed the anti-depressants. She needed him. She needed his ability to keep her distracted from the pain. It was Mother's Day.

Something everyone around her knew about but her. What the hell was she missing? Then she saw her ... the Kensington client in full throttle on her bottom on Clara's husband. She was enjoying the hell out of him and wailing like a beast devours a prey so sultry and gratifying. She had large breasts and long blonde locks and a beautiful frame. Clara watched them for a while like a cat does milk. She saw in her client's face the expression of passion. Love gone mad. She was exhilarated in the full throttle of the moment. Clara wanted to express her disdain and her pleasure of seeing it for the first time. She knew in her soul then that he had been with her before. He knew her and Clara knew her; he had always been calling regarding the Kensington client. He wanted to know her from the inside out and she wanted to devour him. He was filthy rich and she was another Athena—someone who knew the gratification of wealth. She was in that moment devouring Clara's wealth and Clara just watched intently while chewing her gum. She spit it in the toilet and left the condo. She traversed the city blocks that took her there. She stopped at her favorite café. She ordered an iced latte with almond milk and got a cherry danish. She thought about her own gratification in the moment.

She looked around. She observed no one in the moment—none of them aroused in her what she saw in her own bedroom. She felt momentarily that she had not known her mother at all. Norma was harboring secrets. Quinton was harboring secrets. Clara felt those she loved the most had love affairs that were so elusive she found it erotic. She found them more appealing then than the day-to-day of calling about business. In fact, one more business prospect was going to set her off. She left the café. She thought about returning to the cabin. But she didn't. She took the bridge over the bay to New Jersey where she went to their second home. It was large. It was decorated in a coastal white with turquoise blue accents. She put love into that home. She let the home love her back. She lit some candles. She got into the hot tub. She said heck with it and she would let him have her like the toy doll she was. Clara was the trophy prize he paraded around the clients—until the Kensington woman showed up—but they had no prenup. Everything Quinton had he owed to her literally as well as figuratively, and she smiled then like the grim prospect of the Cheshire Cat that knows something no one else knows. And he called. This time she did not answer, and she went to sleep in the king of all king beds. Then she thought about Bella knowing she had to go back to the condo to retrieve her dog, not knowing why she left her there in the first place, knowing too that having left her there certainly told Quinton she had been home.

Chapter Eleven

The keys jingled in the locked door. Quinton opened it with calm composure.

"When did you get home?" He hid it well. "It's only noon. Thought you'd be later." He kissed her.

Clara wondered if he showered. Clearly he brushed his teeth. Thank God.

"I was only here to bring Bella back so I could go to the café."

"Oh yeah? What time?"

"Just an hour ago," she lied.

"Oh okay." She sensed his relief.

She wondered if he just got back from taking the princess home.

"How's everything?"

She didn't tell him Mother's Day was crushing her soul and she missed her mother.

"It's fine."

"Any movement on the Kensington File?"

The Kensington File as they called it was another banking proposition to merge the banks together into one, to enhance profitability rather than compete in the world of banking. Together they would merge and juggle multi-billion-dollar projects like they had done with Enoch's private island. The business deal was huge. Kensington was not just Quinton's mistress but the wealthy owner, Tim Gates' much younger wife. It was all very typical; she married into money to a much older man and found another man to be most pleasurable. Clara saw it in Kens' face like she had never been ravished before. Clara was growing mad. Sinister even. God had taken her only real love being her mother and quite possibly her mother hid the truth from her in the same way she found her husband. It wasn't like being cheated on. It was like being screwed over while having always been the caterer. She was livid. There was going to be one way they took care of her and not themselves. The condo. The house. The cabin. Those were her places of refuge, and she would let them love her back. She would let love live in those places she called home. She would do it and relish in it. She would let love happen.

She moved on past all of it in the months that followed. She worked. She studied. She prospered in the clientele she delivered to Quinton's door. She bought white shag rugs for the foyer and had the house painted and accented. She bought jewelry from the local dealer who purchased only the most exquisite of diamonds.

Then Bella died and she threw herself into the business of making more money than New York City had ever delivered. She walked past Maverick Saint Square on her way to the café. She took her latte to Central Park. She felt the green grass beneath her feet. She considered the idea of being utterly alone as her hallmark. In her mind, she was wealthier than Athena ever dreamed—she was wealthier than the Kensington mistress had ever known. Wealth was her power. She held the hands of New York City's most prosperous well-to-dos with their firm handshakes, and she was commissioned. She took forty percent market share and invested in Wall Street, then opened bank accounts for the elites in the entertainment industry.

She was on fire.

She worked Wall Street. She worked the bank. She worked the hotels. She put the art gallery on ice with her second gallery showing. She was an artist, and in the months that passed she painted vigorously in hues of dark purple and deep red. She had hot cars and fine bed linen. She put herself on the pedestal in the speech she delivered at the gallery.

"Will they appreciate?" a wealthy entertainer said.

"They appreciate like the stock market in the heat of July." She smiled. She re-coiled. She let them know she had money, and she meant business.
Clara hadn't been to the cabin in months. She auctioned her art. She hosted the gallery alongside Vinny who did exceptional photography. She dazzled while she shined and she went to the island to light up the casinos. She drank fine wine and wore exquisite dresses and it was at the grand opening of the Kensington Hotel in New Jersey where Kensington herself showed with her ninety-year-old husband, and Clara had outdone her.

"You can marry into money or be entirely made of money," she said in her divine presence, and the Kensington mistress had eyes large as saucers. Like the moon eclipsed by the sun.

Clara was on fire.

She mingled. She danced. She held hands. She showed a brave face in the midst of immense wealth. Singers and songwriters knew her face.

"I knew she could do it," Quinton told Vinny and Ashley.

Clara rolled her eyes. They didn't see her. She did it all for herself. She marveled in the doing of something for herself. For all the years she nursed her mother but more for having made Quinton money because she would never take back the caring of her mother. And at the end of the day, she went back to the cabin.

Back to the paint. Back to the art she knew would appreciate. Back to the next time Paul and Thomas asked to display her art.

The foliage turned from green to colors of autumn when she made it back to the cabin. She wanted to paint the foliage in hues of red and something sinister lurking in the woods. She showed teeth of wolves or the werewolf of hell who devours the mistress that would only be revealed in abstract contrasts of blackened berries on a twig deep in winter: the leaves fell and the snowfall had her inside. Had her gazing within when she peered out her window mid-stroke and she saw him.

He was rough. Rugged. And well defined. Muscular. It was an unusually warm day in late-fall, and he had no shirt and his shorts were torn. He had some scruff but overall his appearance was captivating. He had long jet-black hair he tied back. He looked native or mixed. He was bronze and average in height. He stepped onto the small front porch. He placed his bag down and took a seat at the only chair available. She opened the door and stood facing him. She was silent at first.

"Oh, hello," is all he could say until she interrupted.

"Who are you, and what are you doing here?"

"I'm sorry," he really didn't answer her question, "I thought someone else might be here."

"Who … someone else?"

"There was a woman … I helped her once."

"You helped her once?"

"I did. She fell."

Clara snapped her head to fling her hair back. The day was warm especially for fall. She wore a buttoned blouse with only her panties underneath.

"You just helped her?"

"I did." He stood looking at Clara.

"You don't think that I…"

"She was my mother."

"*Was* your mother? I'm sorry…"

"She passed two years ago now."

"Hey," he extended his hand. "I'm…"

She lurched forward and stumbled into his arms. He caught her to keep from falling. She looked to his face. His breath smelled like the cherries he had been eating. She smoothed her face down his bare arm and he followed suit. He held her there. They didn't speak. The autumn breeze blew their hair. They began on the porch as she drew her leg up his thigh. He held on to her and ran his hand up her thigh. Then they kissed like lovers do when they are in their first moment together, sultry and subdued. He picked her up fully, and she was led inside in his arms. The Murphy bed was down. She whipped herself around and took his jeans into her teeth as she forced him to the bed. He played along with everything she did. She took his zipper and drew it down. She took off his cargo shorts and stood up.

"Now, I want you to take me like that."

She wasn't settling for another bottom.

He was with her completely. He took her and threw her onto the bed. He ripped her buttons, began at her neck with his mouth and moved down to her panties. She wrapped her legs around him; he took her arms behind her head. He found her exquisite and began to thrust. They kissed madly. It had been too long. He didn't know how long it had been. She didn't care to know. They were enthralled like lovers making it outside beneath a starry sky like a pair of teenagers doing it for the first time—but totally experienced.

She moaned. He thrust and could not hold on to her tight enough. He took her hair back. Her neck was pulsating and he kissed her there and grabbed onto her neck intensely as she was completely giving in to him. Feeling completely wanted. Their desire for one another's bodies was intense. They grew intensely in the moment. She ended lying on her stomach. The feel of him was hypnotic and he let out a powerful sigh and collapsed to the side of her. She was done in the moment. She took a shower. He went outside, pulling up his boxer briefs. He laughed to himself in the moment of feeling exuberant. He returned back inside, collapsed on the bed. He was smitten by the way she took him. The way she wanted him to take her.

With the start of her car, she left him there. She returned home to her immaculate home. Her prestigious life. The man who took her the way she wanted to be wanted—she didn't ask his name. He was a no name. Then she thought about the painting. The closet. Her mother painted him. He was the man in the portrait. Clara laughed. Even her mother thought of him—enough to paint his face. She thought about her mother's portrait, how it was left out in the open, how her mother was there, in that intense moment of heat and passion.

She did not know why she left him there like that, but knowing she had to get back to life eventually anyway. She had his wild and fiery eyes in her mind, and she began to laugh, then she wailed aloud like being given a new car at sixteen. The

114

exuberance was heightened by the idea of him taking her forcefully even if she had to show him. Because otherwise how would he know? He was a gentleman, and she was a lady. The sex and the intimacy before the love gratified her in mind for the next several weeks.

Clara had also left her most recent paintings in the cabin. She knew she would go back. She wondered about him, about how far he had gone, about how he helped Norma once. How Norma was so captivated she painted him. The lines in his face were exquisite along with every tribal tattoo and piercing.

The months turned up with no sight of him. She still had not returned to the cabin. It was two months that had gone by, and Clara prepared for Christmas the way a good wife should do.

"Sweetie, can you pass me the salt?"

Ashley was salting the potatoes.

"I'm going to the store," she told Ashley. "I'll be back before dinner."

"Oh, sure. Everything will take about two hours."

She was on her way to Maverick's toy store when she saw him on the street.

"How are you today?" He was flirting.

Clara sensed he was just trying to manipulate the situation. She thought that he must know about the affair Quinton was having with the Kensington woman. He would not give to her the way the man with no name gave to her. She wanted to know more of him. She thought initially he was a one-night stand. Maybe he was. She then dreaded he might be gone forever. Clara had questions.

"She fell," he had told her.

Then she thought he was her rescuer. Momentarily her knight in shining armor. A man of chivalry. Perhaps Norma loved his face similarly—the way she created him on canvas. Funny how the only paintings left in the cabin were her mother's portrait and the man with no name. They were left in the cabin together. Both seemingly an equal mystery to her.

She tried to force a smile. Maverick was a womanizer.

She decided to walk with him. She thought of the one she left in the cabin. Was she so much different from the womanizer? At that moment she didn't think so.

"How are you, Maverick?"

"I'm always well…"

"Always?"

"My middle name is Saint."

"Literally?"

"Literally. Maverick Saint Square."

"I'm out here," she said

"To Christmas shop I'm sure…"

He opened the door for her, and she stepped through.

Inside was a grand display of all things Christmas. All things a child would enjoy, along with a hefty price tag. They parted ways when she got to the ornaments on the tree that were for sale.

She was distracted.

"Let me know if you ever want to grab something to eat," he kind of hollered at her. "On me."

"I will." She did not turn to look at him.

She found a little mirror in an ornament of a baby's first Christmas. The mirror was beside a slat for a photo of the baby aside the mirror that said, "I'll Always be With You." As the baby aged, he or she would see their own reflection or adversely the mother would see her own through the years of aging.

She thought about how she left him in the cabin. She considered if he was alone through the holiday. She thought about her cheating husband. How their entire social crowd must know. What they must think of her. Clara decided not to care. She wanted to buy the little ornament. So she did. With no one to give it to. She could put Norma's face there aside "I'll Always Be With You."

I'll always miss you, Mom, she thought.

Maverick was in the office conference room. They were expanding. He was also expanding on the West Coast. Washington and Nevada needed a store. He was prospering enough in New York to cover the fortunes of building on the island. Then to branch out in the West. He had a team who were dedicated. Well-paid managers. Maverick Saint Square was also known for his generous donations. The public doted on him.

Clara returned to Ashley's in time for dinner. She brought gifts that were wrapped at the store. She wasn't going to be around Christmas Day—she intended to be at the cabin.

"What's all that?" Ashley inquired.

"Gifts for the kids."

She thought about her own brokenness. Another Christmas without Norma. Another Christmas she intended to do alone in the cabin. Skyla, Raven, and River opened their gifts. It was two days before Christmas. Christmas Day was on a Saturday that year. Skyla unwrapped a dress, matching beads, a necklace, shoes...

"You do too much." Ashley looked to her.

"Never too much." Clara was sincere.

The men watched with bourbon in hand except for Vinny, who had changed for the sake of his family. Clara loved them; she knew she stayed with Quinton for the love she had for Ashley and Vinny. She could not imagine not being their sister-in-law.

Raven opened her gifts and received books and accessories; she was an avid reader.

River opened toys, games, puzzles, and blocks; he loved assembling and Ashley felt he was an aspiring engineer.

Mystique and James arrived mid-opening. Explaining they were sorry to have missed dinner. Mystique was pregnant with a second miracle child; Clara thought briefly that she could potentially have her miracle too.

Ashley kissed her other sister-in-law on the cheek.

"It's okay. We made you plates in case you couldn't make it in time for dinner."

Clara was happy she brought gifts for Trinity too, just in case. James was helping his wife remove her coat. Clara immediately thought about the ornament.

"I think this was meant for you." Clara removed it from her pocket.

Mystique was having a difficult time being pregnant with all the weight she gained. James saw their reflection in the mirror.

"It's beautiful," Mystique said.

"You can put your sonogram in it." Clara thought it was special.

Mystique thought so too.

They were having a boy. Vinny wanted the name Nicholas and chuckled because the baby's due date was near Christmas.

Ashley wondered how Mystique could be there. The doctors would need to induce her soon.

"When are you due?" Ashley was worried.

"Rain will be here December 31st."

Mystique was not going with any other name.

"We have a cesarean scheduled," Vinny said and took Trinity to the table. They were all hungry. After she ate, she opened Clara's gifts. They had hot cocoa for the kids. The adults drank modestly and made sure the kids came first.

Quinton barely spoke a word to Clara. She felt tense around him. Their marriage appeared fine to others while she felt it was on the rocks. She saw a change in him. She felt the change in herself.

If they were not business partners, it might have ended weeks ago. But they had a lot to do, and Clara knew going to the cabin meant she could take a much-needed break. When she got there, he was there. Sitting on the front porch like he had always been there.

Chapter Twelve

"You look like you never left," she said.

She hid her admiration.

"That's because I never did." His smile was charming.

"Don't you have a family?"

He ignored her question at first.

"You wanted to use this bachelor and never see me again?" He was so earnest it hurt.

"Bachelor?"

"I'm not married. Not even widowed."

"Widowed." Widowed was how she felt through it all. Then her intensity arose in her throat. She felt a sensation between a fire and thirst. She went to him; he embraced her on that front porch; the landscape was covered in snow.

She could melt into him. He took and lifted her from the ground.

"I couldn't just let you leave like that," he said. "So I just waited for you."

Her legs were wrapped around him and they kissed passionately like being immensely in love; he used his back to force the door to open. He bumped the canvas portrait.

He tossed her onto the bed. He turned her over. Her lip bled.

"I'm sorry ..." he began.

"Shut up." She swiped her lip. She was wearing a jean jacket over a sweater.

She threw the jacket over Norma. They commenced in foreplay in a deep affection and a love so profound they both had never experienced before. At least she didn't think he did. And she didn't care. She longed for being wanted and his desire for her was hypnotic.

Then Clara saw her. Norma was in plain sight out the window on the front porch and she was smoking a cigarette.

Clara turned her back and he grabbed onto her back and forced his penetration like a mountain lion does the queen of her pride. She was a queen of her throne in their second moment of nearly fatal attraction; they could die together in love. In a deep ravine of maddening sexual attraction. He took the strawberries out of the fridge, the vodka off the shelf. He had gone shopping and had taken up complete residency in the cabin.

Norma sat on the front porch dressed like a summer day and inhaled her cigarette, but she never looked to them. Clara moaned in a voice of sultry sweetness as he salted her naval because he preferred Spanish beer.

She took shots of vodka followed by strawberries. Her lips tasted sweet and spiked with punch. Her lip still bled.

Quinton decided to FaceTime.

"Bit my lip eating a strawberry," she said again as if he didn't hear the first time.

Her lover grabbed a moistened towel.

She ended the call.

She had no desire for chatting over business. So what if it was Christmas Day? He was letting her ride him like a fish in a tsunami. But the tsunami was only turbulent in her own space. In the cabin. Back at the condo it was more like a ripple in a pond— as she thought of the sex with Quinton. She was being patted dry then with another cloth.

She bit his finger. He kissed her again.

He was like a vampire to her; thirsting for her blood he could ravage like a bowl of hot soup. The outside temperature was freezing. The inside was hot, affectionate, and intense.

Norma had disappeared.

Clara looked to him and together they drank while Quinton tried to FaceTime; she would lie to him later.

Clara thought about the painting in the closet. Then she dismissed it, deciding to never take it out of the closet again. Why Norma painted the portrait of her rescuer would be a mystery and she could only determine that Norma found him appealing— and maybe Norma even decided not all men are terrible.

But then Clara had another demise. She walked out to the front porch. She looked down to an ash tray aside the rocking chair.

"Do you smoke?" she said to the man who walked onto the porch.

They did not have a name exchange until that second meeting. Clara took off after their first encounter as a woman who had an affair and a one-night stand. But she was wrong. Hunter Green wanted to see her again. And he took refuge in that cabin like Norma had before them. Clara's refuge became Hunter's place of solitude and she was okay with that. But it seemed that even in death Norma needed the place.

123

"Do you smoke?" she asked again.

"No. Why?"

"Where did this ash tray come from?"

"I don't know. I never noticed it before."

Clara let it go. She didn't know most things about death like most other people. She did however see a light like an aura around her mother made like a silhouette around her body. In death she was younger and more vibrant, and Clara reasoned that she preferred to smoke. Her mother was riddled with arthritis, Parkinson's disease, and then dementia as a woman who had aged. In death she was young again, and vibrant.

She removed the jean jacket from the portrait. She saw in that image her mother's similar face: with no lines and vibrant hues.

She wondered if Norma knew already that death was not just an outcome from aging but also a renewal in what used to be; a life continuum of youth because a moment in time could be captured forever beyond the paint. Beyond the photograph.

The day waned to night and Clara lay in her bed while Hunter talked to her about his life. She learned more about him than any man she had ever met.

He was alone. He had no family. Hunter Green stayed in that cabin because he had nowhere else to go. Clara decided she would stay in their home in New Jersey while allowing Quinton to reside in the condo. They had a broken marriage and they both knew it; Clara had lost Norma and Bella, and her husband was having an affair. But God delivered that holy man named Hunter Green, and they talked while passionately eating strawberries and Clara enjoyed wine between shots of vodka—they would get

124

sick later. She told her husband she'd be home. But she was intoxicated and going nowhere soon.

Hunter delivered in bed. He also ravished her mind; he completed a PhD but left his professorship to travel and take up hiking. The cabin was off his usual path but he heard a woman moaning and found Norma on the steps; Clara thought about showing him the painting to share with him the way her mother must have thought about him, but again she dismissed it. To literally never take her mother's secret from the closet; he would be concealed the same way her mother had done—their thirsty little secret.

Clara listened as he spoke of teaching; chatting about his love of archeology and for digging for ancient artifacts. He had a gift of music too—he could sing with a kind of twang and he played the guitar.

"A rocking guitarist kind of professor." Clara doted on him.

She was madly in love, and she preferred that she would not run away that time.

Her mother's image still burned bright in her mind.

The cigarettes had another effect.

The portrait wasn't concealed but Clara decided in that moment she would take her mother home; she would hang her portrait in the hall. She didn't really know why, but she wanted to have her mother in some way because it was clear her mother preferred her solitude in the cabin, which broke her heart a little. But if her mother would take the cabin in a way, Clara would take having her in the only way she could—as an image of the way her mother was in death rather than the woman who aged in pain.

Hunter discussed his past as having been from a well-off family, as a son of a man who was a renowned neurosurgeon and a mother who could cook. Clara shared her love of vegan cuisine, and he spoke of his love for Spanish food.

She said she dabbled in paint and loved the ocean. Marine life was sacred, she said, and aquatic mammals are equally intelligent beings to humans, she told him.

When they were done conversing over strawberries, wine, lemons, and shots, they lay together entirely spent. He was a romance she didn't know before. He handed her the dry cloth that previously blotted her lip, and she wiped her fingers of the strawberry juice and sugar.

The following morning, he was gone. She stepped onto the front porch and looked, scanning the snowy landscape. She glanced over her shoulder and found an empty ashtray and she went to her Discovery.

She knew the two of them would be a secret. A secret out in the total open expanse before them without having to hide at all.

When she arrived home, Quinton told her they were going to London.

Quinton's family's legacy was extending to Europe and of course he needed his wife on a business trip. It was in London where Quinton and Enoch settled a multi-billion-dollar casino, hotel, bank, and condominium. Money kept making money. Their assets and their investments never faulted, and they were grand as a five star hotel ought to be. They were a power couple. Quinton took his wife to the elegant dinner parties and gave her jewels fit for a princess or the Queen herself. Their money was thick but so was her growing love for the man she felt she knew more than her husband. And, again, her mind traveled back to Hunter Green.

He had been traveling solo on his initial trip to Vermont, and when he went off the beaten path of the Appalachian Trail, he found Norma, who had gone down on her outdoor stairs. That truth resided at the pit of Clara's stomach—what if Hunter hadn't been there that day? Then, what if Clara hadn't discovered the painting? She would never have known that she and her mother had sentiments for the same man. That thought resonated deep within her. That cabin harbored a deep, dark secret and she wore the flashy necklace wondering if she'd see him again soon. She dressed in the morning wondering if he was just waking up at the cabin. She knew he came from money, but he became a kind of adventurer who was okay with not having extravagance. She was thinking that a dark and mysterious bachelor was the finest delicacy she's ever had. She relished and indulged in him. They were both selfish. They thought only of their desire.

Athena, Enoch, and subsequently Quinton created Vegas wherever they went. As one half of a real Power Couple, Clara knew she was there just for looks. She looked good in the eyes of the public. What they had was superficial at best.

The third night with Hunter in the cabin became the most intense, and the heat and passion was heightened; they resided in the cabin together at the turn of the New Year, and they stayed together in that cabin as if they knew no one else.

"Do you like fish?" he asked her.

"No, hence, vegan." She laughed.

"No, I mean, you wanted to study oceanography, right?"

"Oh." She laughed again. "Yes, I adore those little guys."

Her eyes could bore holes in his skin. She licked the sugar from his fingers because she preferred sugar on the rim of her margarita than salt.

127

"Why sugar?"

"It complements the mango."

Sweet and sultry was their style. She drank her mango margarita and wondered why he liked most things Spanish.

Then she thought of his dark skin and jet-black hair.

"You're Spanish too?"

"That's right. I am."

"I didn't think the accent..."

"It's not Spanish. I know. My mother however is Spanish and my father is Italian."

"And yet you never eat pasta."

"My mother was the cook."

"That's right."

"My father was from Sicily, but he studied here in the states and my mother's family emigrated here several generations ago."

"I would love to meet them."

That was out of context for the situation, but he played along.

"They would love to meet you, Clara."

They couldn't help but indulge in their secret.

To meet his parents was a step only three nights in the cabin didn't necessarily merit.

She liked the idea of knowing him the way he knew Norma. No man outside of Quinton knew Norma and although Quinton was outwardly tolerant, she knew the façade of patience was his best falsity. Quinton just thought he should be liked by everyone because he was filthy rich. But not Norma. Norma knew better; she knew a fake man more than anyone and she was able to get deeper beyond his striking appearance being like the rock and roll legend.

Looking like Elvis appealed to most women Norma's age and Clara felt that one day Quinton would grow on her but that never happened. She was intrigued initially by his looks and decided from there that men were still not worth it. Then she painted the portrait of Hunter Green.

"Did she know your name?" Clara said and thought she smelled a cigarette.

"So she never mentioned me?" He appeared a bit sullen.

Chapter Thirteen

She didn't know what to say.

Then she just gave it to him matter-of-factly.

"No. My mother was abused by men."

That damn painting threw her off.

"But I think she thought highly of you."

"Well, if she didn't mention me..."

"She didn't have to. She was an artist. She only painted the things that inspired her."

"Wait, you mean she painted me?"

She thought about the painting in the closet. The painting she wanted to leave there to never take out again.

Because he was Norma's secret.

"She did."

"But she never said anything?"

"She did not."

"Can I see it? I mean is it here?"

"No."

"No? No to which one?"

"Both."

"Ouch."

"She didn't want me to know she fell. She never wanted me to bring her to New York to live."

"That's it then. She lived with you in New York."

"I live in New Jersey now."

"Your husband?"

"He's having an affair. He has a mistress. Melody Kensington is her name."

"You know her name?"

"Yes. She's our client."

"Client?"

"I am the director of the bank."

She realized then how little he knew her.

"You only told me what you wanted to do..."

"And not what I do. But now you know. I run a bank."

"And you moved to New Jersey?"

"We own a house there."

"So he stays in New York..."

"While I stay in New Jersey."

"Does he know you know?"

"We both just don't care."

"What exactly would you like to do?"

"Pickles and relish." She moved the sheet up her thigh.

"You mean like sloppy seconds?"

She slapped him. "I mean like toppings on your hotdog sir."

"Since you called me sir..."

"Sir..." she was like a vixen.

He yielded to her.

"Ma'am." He took her between his teeth. Gently at first. Harder then. And her eyes rolled back. It was like Phantom of the Opera in the cabin.

"It hurts a little," she said of his teeth.

He let go.

She took his hair between her fingers.

He grappled at her neck.

He took her then.

She was the one yielding.

They moved together in a rhythm of blues and jazz. He held her like he did when he strummed his guitar—she imagined.

Blues summed up her life without Norma. Momma was special. Jazz was the finesse Clara's kind of somber tone needed.

Then Norma appeared again. She was a breeze walking past the window.

"Momma," Clara said.

Hunter looked to the window and back to Clara.

"Is someone out there?" He was unnerved.

"No," she said and took her hand up his solid buttocks and was thrilled at the heightened climax some paranoia can evoke during sex. Like the height of adrenaline telling the body to fight or take flight.

He went to the door after he hiked up his pants. The temperature was above freezing that night. He saw no one. In that moment he felt concerned.

"Are you okay?" he said.

"I am now." She meant it.

The power behind sex was the kind of distraction a broken soul yearned for in her case. Her own power was the energy she felt being completely wanted and it was even better when he wanted no one else. She was beautiful in flesh and in that split second, she revealed her soul.

Clara wanted him back.

She thought about Quinton. She thought about divorce. About taking up her place in the cabin, but she didn't know if Hunter could live with a ghost. Why hadn't her mother crossed over? Clara couldn't reason with Norma not having a party in Heaven with Helen and Lucille. If her solitude meant so much then perhaps Clara was being asked to leave. Her mother never looked at her. She was rightfully engaged in adult therapy. She reasoned that sex was as much a therapy as was smoking a cigarette. When she was able to collect herself and gather her things, she piled her luggage into her Discovery and kissed Hunter Green before she departed.

She was on her way to visit Ruby.

When she arrived, she felt exuberant. She yearned to tell her everything. Ruby aged more gracefully than Norma had and at seventy-eight she still lived alone and cared for herself.

"I see Mom," she told her.

Ruby wasn't surprised, or if she was, she didn't show it.

"Where do you see your mother?"

"At the cabin."

"How?"

"Smoking a cigarette."

"You're back to smoking?"

"No, Mom is."

"You see Norma smoking cigarettes in the cabin?"

"Outside."

"Isn't it a bit cold? And when do you see her?"

"During sex."

"I'm sorry?"

Clara looked to Ruby and told her everything she experienced from Quinton's affair to her prowess for male attention.

Quinton's affair didn't shock Ruby either.

"Because men are no good," she said. "But why don't you put your energy into art?" she said of the man in Clara's life.

Clara shouldn't have been surprised, but she was.

She thought about abstract art. About the tones of blue and gray that mirrored her emotions of her mother's ailing body and later her mind.

Art wasn't all inclusive. What she felt with Hunter was primal. She didn't fear him; she didn't fear the forceful nature of being utterly wanted.

She returned to the cabin to find him gone.

Hunter was mysterious, nomadic, and pretty unpredictable. She liked that. They both came and went as they pleased. She felt free. She had a man in her cabin that she could claim all to herself; she kept the same man Norma kept in the closet to herself. They had that in common. Norma was as wild as she was, Clara thought, and she went home to New Jersey. She gathered her things. She intended to leave him entirely, but something for a moment didn't feel right. She looked about that New Jersey house and found nothing unusual. The sensation of being watched or followed crept up on her. She had an impulse to call Hunter, but she had never gotten his number or ever inquired if he had a phone in the first place.

Her cellphone rang. It was Quinton. He had previously chosen FaceTime because she thought he actually wanted to see her face, but she learned the Kensington mistress occupied his time in that condo by Central Park. She missed Bella in that moment too; she missed Hunter's peering brown eyes behind long dark hair. She loved his Spanish flair and his Italian physique like he gave credence to the tall, dark, and mysterious lover.

She wanted more. How much more she wasn't sure. But she wanted to find out. Clara gathered all that she could. She took a laptop computer because she would help the jerk while she could tolerate him, but she would strategically phase herself out of his business, out of her mother-of-puns' affairs and to never experience him sexually again.

Clara Wood was unstoppable. She was going to take complete control of her life and when she decided to get to it, she launched her best clothes into that Discovery and she drove back to the cabin.

Back to Hunter Green.

When she arrived, there was a woman on the porch. Clara reasoned that she might be another through-hiker. Then Hunter stepped outside and was waving like a woman on a float. She chuckled. He looked cute.

"Hi," the woman said with a smile.

"Hi." Clara was warm.

"I'm Cindy," she began. "Here…" she nudged him. "I'll let you introduce us."

"She's my mom." He had this youthful kind of innocence about him.

136

"Hello, I'm Clara." She darted her hand in a warm shake and Cindy gave her a hug.

Clara felt the introduction was a bit like "the other woman" to her but she did figure she was his only woman. No harm done.

"I brought her back," Hunter explained.

"I'm an avid hiker myself but this weather is too cold."

"Let's go inside." Clara led the way.

Inside there was a wonderful aroma and she noticed a tart burner.

"It's kind of like a housewarming gift." She was sweet.

Cindy had an athletic body, and she talked to Clara about her family's move to the U.S. and how her mother was a Spanish migrant who met her father, who was an ordinary dairy farmer. Hunter had a thick Spanish background she met Hunter's father abroad while she studied French. He taught her Italian and she taught him Spanish.

"Hunter didn't tell me he was fluent in multiple languages."

"Hunter doesn't tell many things."

Clara thought of his portrait in the home she left behind feeling like she should have grabbed it on her way out the door. It was left to Quinton's finding and she didn't like that. Or worse yet, Athena's finding. She didn't want to be the demon in Quinton's life, but his extra-marital affair left her with no choice, and the man of her dreams had appeared on her doorstep—a man whose image captivated Norma so much that she remembered him at least visually despite the onset of dementia. As far as Clara was concerned, she shared that man with her mother. That painting bridged a gap between them. Her mother was not entirely put off by all men; she painted one, and only the things that captivated her most she would bother with painting. Just like Clara painted her mother. That image stays within the cabin. It is home to her mother in life and in death in more ways than one.

She didn't find it peculiar that she saw her mother. She knew how much the cabin meant to her mother. Her solitude wasn't formidable and neither was her penchant for art, so the two combined in that beautiful environment was therapeutic—it was no wonder to Clara that she would return. Clara wasn't averse to being near her mother despite their inability to communicate; Norma was living in an angelic form on a different frequency than the living. Clara felt she understood that the body remains while the soul departs, but she thought too that her mother would like to be among the previous generation of women. She imagined being able to give Norma the fifth baby girl, but that time had passed she believed. She wasn't averse to knowing Cindy either but also wondered how she would feel regarding her mother's appearances; it did not appear anyone else could perceive that level of energy.

Cindy stayed over the weekend. It occurred to her that Quinton wouldn't know that she left. They lived apart anyway. They didn't discuss the fact that Clara was still married of course. She considered herself separated the moment she found the Kensington client in full straddle over her husband—they had only been together a decade. Clara was loyal to everyone and she felt the betrayal and mistrust would always keep them apart. Hunter filled that void. Cindy's gregarious personality won her heart. Then she asked about the painting.

"She's beautiful." Cindy smiled sweetly.

"Thank you. That's my mother, Norma."

"Named after superstars."

138

"She was. Norma Jean Wood."

"You miss her like I miss my mother, I'm sure."

"I do." Clara smiled back.

Clara wondered why Hunter was so eager to bring Cindy out to the cabin; then Cindy answered her question as if reading her mind...

"Hunter wanted me to meet you like he got to meet your mother."

Norma's portrait was facing them. Clara eyed the painting and answered, "I'm happy to meet you and I do love that Hunter was able to help my mother."

Chapter Fourteen

Norma had a memory of her daughter's face when Clara would show her paint. The art would trigger something inside her. Then Clara wondered why her mother would choose cigarettes over art—as if they both didn't agree with one another's choices. Norma had chosen art over people for most her life aside from Clara and Ruby. She didn't take to Quinton despite his charm. She did paint a man of chivalry and they shared that in common— they were both inspired by the same man. Hunter lit a candle inside the cabin. The weekend neared the end and Cindy went home. Norma lit a smoke outside the window. Clara undressed and beneath her skirt she wore red laced panties without stockings. He slipped one hand up her skirt...

"I'm going to treat you like a bar girl." He played along.

He took a piece of ice from the cooler. He put it in his mouth until it turned subtly to water and removed it. Hunter Green slid that piece of ice up her thigh and they made out like that all spring with every chance they had.

His shirt was torn from the aggression. That time her lip did not bleed. She flung her hair, and he grabbed on to her. Her neck was like candy to his very cool mouth that still remained like ice to her body. The portrait was turned around, but Norma showed up to smoke a cigarette outside on the porch beside the window.

The snow had long gone. Quinton and Clara accepted their separation, which was only by distance and not by legalities. Spring nursed the environment to a budding landscape, and she painted the petunias and peonies and every other flower as they traveled.

She traveled with his hands in mind when they were not having sex. She thought about his muscular body and dimples. Elvis had nothing on Hunter Green.

140

Clara ate peaches from his fingers and sucked his pointer with a sultry flair. They were inconsolable in the bedroom—"Give me more," he made her say and he would thrust from behind—he just couldn't handle any less of Clara Wood.

Norma never said a word to Clara about Hunter. She figured Norma would have said something if it caused concern. Clara didn't bring Norma to New York until the dementia became severe. Norma only understood that she needed continuous care, and in the end she could only ask for waffles with chocolate. She didn't know Clara by name at that point and Norma lost her memories completely. Being outside the window smoking a cigarette brought an old comfort back that Clara had long gotten past. They quit smoking together and they never looked back. That cigarette was a token of the past—when things were okay— a time before the arthritis in her hands. Clara wondered why her mother had so many ailments.

With Hunter she forgot all that. And she was comforted with the visits from her mother. At the time, all things were okay. She could have them to herself there in that remote little space.

Clara liked Hunter. She loved his hand on her thigh. The way he took off her string bikini with his teeth and how he used his mouth on her neck. They danced naked in the rain outside that cabin. He gave her pleasure that she had never known had she not shown him. They were the cat's meow together. Naked at the table they ate strawberries and whipped cream.

Quinton called, always about business, and they simply accepted one another's distance. She was still making him money. She worked remotely. It was all too easy. Hunter sold everything he owned to take up hiking the Appalachian Trail and never went back to insurance policies and taxes. Like Norma he took refuge in the cabin. Clara had the greatest of both worlds.

She had money and sex and all the financial freedom Hunter Green sought but only in a different way. Hunter's father did brain surgery while Hunter decided a more nomadic life was his cup of tea (or whiskey). Clara wanted his punctuality and reliability; those qualities the wealthy didn't necessarily have; they had a high-end status that made them superior. She indulged in his centerfold-worthy physique and they could have been on the cover of the magazines together, as sexy as they were together. He would lie spent in her arms and she would stroke his hair. Their cravings went beyond sex when they lay together naked while talking extremist methods to defy the political construct. She would listen to his side of the story—of needing to break away and soar high like a bird. Clara thought about spreading her wings and descending into the ocean.

"Why don't we go to the beach?" he said, without a clue as to how he'd afford the trip with his status of cashless remittance as his only means of payment; he paid her in sex for room and board. She hit his shoulder and told him to shut up. They kissed passionately like two lovers who were madly obsessed with one another's bodies. They were sexy.

They took their sex to the beach. They sat by candlelight at the tiki bar. They danced naked again in the hut that made them feel simplistic and utterly satisfied. There was no breaking them. She didn't have to talk percentages and decimal places. She didn't have to negotiate and ask for one more payment and another signature on the dotted line. She was Clara Wood with Hunter Green and he fed her cherries from her Pina Colada.

They were at Daytona Beach and an impending tornado stirred them, so they had sex by the beach, and he thrust within her as slick and sleek as the red-hot Ferrari beside them. They found an unlocked car and unleashed the beast inside them.

No one had to agree with them. They didn't ask for acceptance. Clara spotted Norma by the water—no doubt she would have decided to paint by the water. Clara paid for everything with her husband's money; if he was going to have an affair, ironically, the last thing she was going to do was divorce him. So she painted Hunter by the ocean. She made him grand. The waves crashed behind him and she thought he looked like a god. She named him Atlas. He was dark and sinister. She was pale like the moonlight. They were opposites to the on-lookers. They were beautiful. She was happy. He was too. She painted the lines of his body in rich detail unlike her mother wanted her to do—unlike Norma had done. His portrait was of an impression from memory. Clara had the sake of rich detail. Norma sat by the ocean—a woman on the beach with a subtle glow. She watched the waves come crashing in. She didn't smoke. She watched. She observed the water of high tide before her, the way she would have done in life. Her hair didn't blow in the breeze, though, the way Norma would have enjoyed when she was alive. The least she could do was to paint him in exquisite detail as she had experienced him with her whole mouth—if only she could paint how he tasted.

"What brought on the sexual prowl-ness?" He crawled to her.

Was it Norma? The dementia? The affair? she wondered and lay in the sand beside him.

"There is no energy more raw than being wanted."

"Oh, I want you, Clara. For sure I want you."

"Yes?"

"There's no doubt about that."

He looked to her artwork.

"It looks like a photograph."

He was impressed.

143

Clara could paint as well as her mother.

"My mother enjoyed meeting you. She wants to have us for dinner next weekend."

"I want you for dinner," she said.

"That's not what I meant." He laughed.

"It's what I mean." She loved to toy with him.

"Right here on the beach?"

"Why not?"

"God how I wish right now, Clara."

She nodded her head—their room was on the beach.

He carried her. They shut out the world behind that door.

He ran the bath water to rinse off the sand. He lit the candles. She burned incense about the room.

He removed her bikini top. Then he removed her bottoms. He carried her again and placed her salty body into the warm jacuzzi they had in their suite. He seduced her the way she wanted. Always intentional and refined the way a sexual encounter should be. She wanted his hands at her neck. He took a step back and rushed in to take her on the towels placed on the floor.

"It's not that you want to kill me," she said, "but you want no one and nothing else."

"I want no one but you, Clara."

They fed one another strawberries (always strawberries) and drank Champagne.

The summer passed by with more indulgences than the two of them had known.

Clara didn't visit Cindy. She always had an excuse. It's not that she didn't like her—quite the contrary—but those days for her had closed. She had already gotten to know a mother-in-law and hadn't been wanted since she never did conceive. She didn't dislike Athena either, because she did get it, and she very much loved Vinny and Ashley—James and Mystique too, but without a child she didn't feel she fit in. So she had a man who desired her and when she was feeling thirsty she ravished him—more often he ravished her. Clara was content in the beauty of their sexual relationship and didn't want another one going south. She was high. And not feeling low was a better place than all the money in the world had been. When Clara wasn't feeling satisfied, she would paint. She would work too. Quinton called and she was there to seal the deal. She was mortified by his texts that went on about, "Why did you just walk away from us?" and she wondered if he was on to a new mistress yet. Sometimes the calls would be frequent, and other times they stopped altogether.

She also had interactions with Maverick Saint Square and the Kensington husband called too. Clara considered that Quinton might fall apart if she leaked the truth. She decided not to tell him a word. Quite matter-of-fact, Clara just didn't care. She had already been ostracized for not giving them a baby. She stopped caring then. She didn't want the affair to be potentially ruined by Cindy too. Or anyone else for that matter. Hunter Green was all hers—together they didn't get lost in the taboo of marriage and spawn to carry on the family namesake—they were together strictly for the pleasure they found in each other's company. She didn't want to ruin that.

Then Clara went home. On her ride home she got a text: *Who's the guy in the painting on the wall?* She didn't respond. She didn't know why really, and she didn't know why she should. Instead, she told him later as she faced him in their Jersey home.

"It's my mother's," she said. "Only she would know."

The whole moment was awkward.

She didn't care if he knew she knew about the affair; she had Hunter Green alone in the cabin. She had gone back to Jersey for the painting. She wanted to show him how her mother must have felt about him—that he was worth the time to paint. In Norma's world, that meant a lot. Everything in the house looked the same.

"We've been distant recently," he said.

"Yeah." She was stuck inside the home they purchased together and with the man she wanted hung on the wall. "If you consider the last six months recent," she told him. "Like it's been three weeks, but whatever."

"I'm happy to see you."

"Well good."

"Do you want to go out to dinner?"

"No."

"What did I do?"

"Nothing."

"What's happened?"

"Just time and space."

146

She walked past him.

He followed her. She removed the painting from the wall; Hunter was a beautiful sight with his long jet-black hair and the physique of a Greek God.

"I saw you with her." She decided to be frank. She also decided she had absolutely nothing to lose.

"How do you know it was me you think you saw?" He almost stuttered but maintained composure.

"It was our bed. Your ass and her. I think I know."

"That's why you didn't stay…"

"You soiled my micro cotton sheets, you asshole."

"I get it…"

"You get what?"

"Not wanting to be here after…"

"No, I didn't want to intrude on your relationship."

"I'm sorry, but relationship… you must understand how hard it was."

"How hard what was?"

"Norma …"

"Being sick?"

"We hadn't been together in a long time…"

"I don't need the pity or the excuses."

"Look, I'm sorry."

"Don't be."

He tried to be earnest but sucked at it.

"I loved you always…"

She left a trail of words behind her. That's all they were—words. Words without emotion. She was feeling free then and knew that woman had been in her bed—a bed of linen she washed and folded. That condo was soiled of the whole smell of it.

She had tried retreating to the house in Jersey that really never felt like a home. Nothing could feel like the cabin.

When she returned to her humble abode in the woods, she smelled cigarette smoke, and that old ashtray still sat empty on the table beside the chair. Norma wasn't visible. Clara would otherwise mistake her for being alive if she had. Hunter was not there. The house sat empty without a single soul around. It felt empty that way too. She hung the painting on the wall awaiting his arrival. At morning, the sun shone through the window and the faint smell of cigarette smoke still permeated her nostrils.

She stepped outside onto her front porch and fall was near. Hunter still had not shown. Clara decided to worry, and despite all the devices she had available, she could not locate a Cindy Green. She had never thought of asking for a last name. She could have been like Norma and maintained a maiden name. A named damned by the person who gave it to her.

Winter settled and she had no word from Hunter. She screamed into her pillow for never having gone to see Cindy. So she went to see Ruby. On the door was a note left by court officials: Notice of Sale pending.

Clara had been so wrapped up into Hunter Green that she hadn't paid a visit to Ruby in so long. Possibly too long. Where the hell was she to go? Clara sat on the porch and snowflakes began to descend upon her nose.

Another Christmas was coming near and those she loved most were nowhere to be found. She scoured the local trails for signs of Hunter. She called the paper. She searched on all channels of local media. She could not for the life of her figure out where he was and had been and why he didn't show again. She had lost her best friend, and she stared at the painting of the man she thought she knew. Then she stole a glance toward her mother—with all that had been happening, where was Norma now?

The smell of cigarettes went out the open windows. She screamed aloud, but only the birds wrestled. She could not stay there at the cabin in the middle of the impending blizzard for fear of cabin fever if she did, so she returned to the house to gather her things, and she left Jersey for an apartment in the bustling city to take her mind off whatever might have happened to Hunter Green.

She was furious at the coming of another Christmas. She was without the love she had, and she took solace with her paint and settled into her new and utterly vacant life wondering if he would return to her once the snowfall had settled. Vermont was experiencing a storm, and the accumulation was several feet thick, so she was happy she had decided not to stay. She went out into the city and found Maverick Saint Square's Toy Shop, was bustling and she entered to find Maverick in passing and decided to say hello.

"Hello again, old friend," he said, "what brings you here?"

A young woman. Blonde. Joined his arm.

"I'm browsing for Christmas gifts." She forced a smile.

"Definitely check out the Giovanni Sculpture sometime."
Maverick had a toothpaste kind of smile. Those glistening white,
ceramic-like teeth.

"I will," she said and moved along.

She wanted to return to the cabin. She wanted to return to
Hunter's embrace and strong arms. She watched Maverick leave
and when she turned back to see, she realized the back of that
woman's head was the Kensington woman with clothes on. And
then she realized, too, that Quinton's multi-billion dollar deal had
fallen through the day before—and life had all its peculiar
synchronicities.

"That woman only screws for money," Clara heard from someone
behind, and she wondered if they were referring to the same
woman.

Was she a prostitute? Clara sniggered and giggled a bit out loud.

And Clara turned over in her bed that night with thoughts of
Hunter. Thoughts of how she never paid her visit to Ruby one last
time and how she still hadn't filed for a divorce from Quinton,
and she wondered further why he hadn't filed either.

Chapter Fifteen

She also hadn't seen Ashley and Vinny in some time. They were so busy that the occasional text went south. Clara picked up her phone and began to search the obituaries. Nothing came up. Hunter Green was MIA and she wondered if he lost his way at some point on the trail—but he was an avid explorer and extremely intelligent. Surely he was okay. She was angry that he was so nomadic and his decisions to hike alone derailed her from thinking all would be well. The cabin was empty. Ruby was buried near Norma as they both had evidently put into their will, because Clara was contacted by an attorney; she was the recipient of Ruby's estate and what she had left of a life insurance policy: $75,000. She took the money and opened a case with the local law enforcement of Vermont. She reported Hunter missing. He wasn't present online at all and the search led to nothing. She still didn't have Cindy's last name and the local law enforcement told her that she didn't know if he actually went missing or if he just didn't want to be found, but they were willing to file a report on the vague information she gave them. She went to bed in the cabin broken and sobbing. Quinton sent a FaceTime as if their relationship wasn't sour and downright spoiled.

"I usually get a call from the wife, not the other way around," the private detective said from her cellphone. "Those guys usually have a spouse and kids back home." But he wasn't going to turn down a deal.

Clara ended the call. She knew Cindy wouldn't show up to the mistress's cabin in the woods. She wanted to believe she meant more than that to him. But did she?

Her mind was spinning.

The paintings sat on their easels, and she thought she'd go mad. And her mother's spirit was nowhere in sight. The empty ashtray sat beside the rocker on the front porch, and she took it and threw it against the outdoor wall. It was thick glass and landed in a heap on the fall foliage.

Christmas was spent in a bitter kind of resentment that made Clara realize she could have gone to his mother's if she could have let go entirely of her commitments; he had been a breath of fresh air in a way she was yearning for since Norma had passed away. He was exhilarating, but for some reason he had gone for a weekend trip into the mountains of Vermont and hadn't come back.

"You said you'd always come back," she whispered to a portrait that couldn't talk back.

She sent a text to Ashley who responded quickly.

"I'm sorry we've lost touch," was her message.

Like all her messages, it was vague and somewhat final. There were no open questions; once she had children, the two of them became busy. The family trips lessened, and Athena was aging. She and Enoch took up refuge in Hawaii where they built a hotel and decided to stay six months out of the year, before deciding they were too old for so much time away from family.

Now, they were close to Vinny and the grandbabies while Clara failed in that department. She wasn't just ostracized but forgotten altogether.

"When are you just going to hang it up and file for a divorce?" Ashley wrote in a text message that Clara assumed was meant for Quinton. She didn't respond.

Instead, she spent that lonely holiday in the cabin entirely sullen while contemplating what to do next. Her solace was in vain. Clara grew in anger and remorse and couldn't shake the feeling of desertion that consumed her. She stopped working. She went to

152

the night club; she felt lost and aging too. Those years she had spent in money were being replaced with solitude and despair.

All she could think to do was to leave. Travel. Go nomadic the way Hunter Green would have done and find herself again.

So, when the New Year passed, she took off. On foot. Up the trail toward the North where snow would abound, but she was feeling the exertion of perseverance, and she left the cabin. Left the portraits to be together in their memories. Clara Wood took to the Appalachian Trail where she could find answers.

Two days into her journey, she felt like she could die. Her feet were frozen and she hadn't eaten in a few days. Her stomach churned and her legs ached. But she was determined and bullheaded and found a small shelter on the walk—an abandoned hunting cabin that she figured he must have seen in her own cabin and the reason he stopped there. Once inside the dingy old cabin she found some kerosene and an old pack of matches. She built a fire; her days with Norma were coming back to her; her childhood playing out through memories of the cabin, once Norma had felt safe to take her daughter there. Clara took out a notebook and began journaling letters to Hunter Green, telling him of her journey—her life growing up among the wild and beautiful wilderness of West Virginia and Vermont; she related in those pages how she would take control of her life in the formative days of becoming a strong woman; she had the power and the energy of the woman who was wanted and desired in ways she gathered most don't experience.

"You offered your hands when I had long been empty," she wrote.

She smiled then and felt compelled to sketch alongside her letters.

She drew the cabin and its rustic appearance, and she intended to show him her journey of becoming a pioneer—trailblazing a path for women who had experienced loss. She didn't regret a moment she spent with him and she hoped that one day she would find him on that trail because certainly he went nomadic again. He left to journey into the life of a warrior and she admired his need for survival—the kind of need that was instilled in him was also the need in her to be wanted so thoroughly by a man. She wanted to tell him in those pages that he was her stimulus and she understood his tenacity when blazing a path for others to follow. In a way she wanted others to know Hunter Green the way she had known him—and she wanted him to know that she yearned for his body and his warmth and she never wanted him to leave.

Still, she couldn't stop thinking back over all her decisions from the last several weeks. Clara had only returned to Jersey to pick up the painting. He told her he'd be out on the trail for the weekend.

But why hadn't he returned?

Chapter Sixteen

That spring, Clara renounced her position of monetary wealth and slept outside under the starry night sky. She felt like she could feel her mother's soul. She couldn't shake the thought of *where are you* and she wanted answers. Clara was alone and the solo trip made her feel powerful; his method of madness made sense to her. Hunter left the wealth he knew as a child and gained an energy that was far more exhilarating—being alone and relying on survival. Going rogue had its intensity and she was thirsty. She was ravenous and the unadulterated pleasure in the outdoors made her feel close to him.

Then she spotted a couple who appeared to be in their thirties. They hiked with light gear and stopped when they saw Clara.

"Hiking alone?" the man asked.

"I'm doing it solo," she replied.

"How far have you hiked?"

"It's my first day."

"Sweet," the woman said. "I'm Tami and this is my husband, Dave." They extended their hands in a warm hello.

"Nice to meet you. I'm Clara."

"That's cool, Clara, we saw your name in a book log back there."

Clara thought to herself, *What the heck are they talking about? Because* she hadn't filled out a book log.

"Book log?"

"It looked like you signed in as a guest in the trail log book," Tami explained.

"They have one about every thirty miles or so," Dave explained. "No matter, are you hungry or thirsty? We have some food."

"We're missing an Instant Pot," his wife joked.

"I would love a hot cup of coffee." Clara was hopeful.

"You're in luck! We have instant coffee." Tami's smile was infectious.

They parked themselves by a large pond and watched the geese alongside their chicks. It was April and the sun was bright.

Clara hadn't seen Hunter in months. She hadn't talked to Quinton in months. She hadn't seen another soul in months. Dave and Tami were the first bodies she crossed since she left the cabin to find the trail. The solitude was getting to her and she needed to stretch her wings and fly away—or die alone in that cabin while waiting for him to return. She decided to venture and look for her nomadic man who took her body into his strong arms and stole her heart.

They sipped coffee. They watched the geese. They chatted about being on the trail for the first time.

"How far you hoping to go?" Dave inquired.

"All the way," was her response.

"You're going north...it's good weather now. You've chosen the right season."

Clara hadn't planned that far ahead.

"I'm not sure about doing it alone." Tami was serene.

"Did you hear about the body?" Dave continued.

"The body?" Clara was dutifully perplexed.

"Someone hiking alone maybe. We don't really know," Tami explained.

"What are you talking about?"

"We don't mean to scare you or anything."

"We're just saying that accidents happen."

"But I still don't know what you're talking about."

"Someone was found in the river is all. Could be unrelated."

Clara sipped her coffee while wondering what the hell they were talking about. People die all the time and they certainly wash up in bodies of water. She thought the trail was pretty straightforward. She didn't feel alarmed in the least.

"Would you like to hike with us?" Tami nodded.

"It's okay. I think I'll be all right."

"The offer is on the table if you change your mind."

"Do you want to hang out tonight and set up camp?" Tami questioned.

"Set up camp here? Now?" Dave looked tired.

"Sure," his wife said and punched his shoulder knowing he would like the opportunity to read a good book.

"You're welcome to stay," Tami said.

"I think I'm going to keep going on for a while." Clara appreciated the offer.

Clara kept a pace she thought was worthy of bragging rights. She still had some of the inheritance Ruby left her and she managed to hitchhike during periods of needing to eat or get some rest. She met a man named Donald who at age seventy bought a gas station that also housed a small service station. Donald treated her to a lemonade and a sandwich. She bunked for the night in a hotel. She watched TV. She did all she could to stay distracted until she screamed into her pillow. She had two cabins to return to at the end of the six months it took to hike that trail from Vermont to Mount Katahdin, Maine. There she met a wealthy executive who offered to take her home. His name was Kevin. Kevin liked Clara for her tenacity to hike the A.T. alone.

"I didn't start out in Georgia," she said, "like the others."

Kevin owned car dealerships and showed her his Bentley, and he was sleazy. She felt bitter resentment at being in his presence and she wondered if she ever appeared that way when she had money. She declined his offer and turned to her savings, investments, and retirement funds.

Clara had money. A lot of money.

She bought a shiny little convertible and went home before the snow could start all over again.

Eventually, after another year, she got a call from the P.I. she hired.

"You sitting down?" he said.

"No." She wasn't joking.

"Very well. The guy you gave me information about wasn't all that honest, but I'll let his mother decide what to tell you unless you want to hear it all from me?"

"No." She hung up and wired him the money.

It had taken him two years to come up with the leads he needed to hunt down Hunter Green.

Clara took a deep breath. She called the number he provided her.

And it was Cindy who answered.

"Hello. Clara?" she said.

"Yes." She was low. Clara had a seat finally.

"Clara, I didn't know how to contact you. You don't exist online. Social media or anything."

"I know. Neither does Hunter."

"No. He wasn't into being known, Clara. He told you his last name was Green." She paused. "Like the color. Hunter thought it was funny. So he changed his name, but not legally. Hunter's father was Anthony Williams, and Hunter had the same name. He didn't like his father, and they never agreed on anything. Hunter didn't view himself as someone like his father. His father was a good man most of the time, but he also worked a lot and wasn't around much. My husband passed away last June, Clara, a year after my son was found in the river."

"The river," Clara asked, her voice breaking.

"Yes. He liked to kayak, but he didn't make it out of the jetty. He drowned, Clara, when he attempted the class six rapids. He'd always wanted to do it. I was against it, but Hunter never did listen. They pulled his body out of the water three weeks later. He was swollen. Bloated. And he wasn't someone who looked like my son. But listen, I tried to find you. You see, he was going to catch up with you after spending the day on the river. He bought you a ring. He wanted to give it to you. I have it. If you'd like to have it, I can give it to you."

Clara's voice broke again, and she shed tears for the finality that became of Hunter Green.

"Yes," she said faintly. "I'll come to you for it."

Clara did that. She went to Cindy's new home in Cincinnati where she had returned to be with family after experiencing the loss of a son and a husband.

Clara told her about the hike she made when Hunter never returned to her.

"He would have returned Clara." Cindy was sincere. "My son was such an adventurous soul."

"He was." She took a breath.

"Would you like to go to his grave?"

"Yes." Clara didn't talk much.

They went to the small family church beside the home where Cindy grew up. She chose to bury Hunter there as well as her husband in a more private lot in that little church. Clara felt God. She felt a chill up her spine. They made it there in May when the day lilies were in bloom.

Cindy turned to Clara in front of her son's grave and gave to her the ring Hunter chose for her.

"He wanted to tell you about his life."

"It's beautiful," she said.

And Cindy had more to share as she removed a stack of binders from her bag.

"He recorded his adventures in these books." She looked pleased.

"You may enjoy them."

"Thank you." Clara was solemn and thankful for that moment with Cindy after she hoped for so long for closure.

"You hiked that trail?" She was proud. "He's so proud of you, Clara."

"I hope so."

They embraced. And Clara returned to her cabin in Vermont. She removed those paintings from the easel and went to Jersey.

She headed there not knowing if the house was still theirs. She was essentially estranged from her husband who she never divorced, and when she got there the lights were still on. To her knowledge the house could not be sold without her signature. The key still worked. She entered her home and found him in the bedroom.

She threw open the door. He was there, in the bed she used for comfort, and his woman looked disgruntled.

"Who the hell?"

Quinton spoke to Clara for the first time in two years.

"He chose me!" Clara yelled at him. "He chose me!"

She threw him the ring he bought for her in their tenth year of marriage."

"Who are you talking about, Magnolia?"

Magnolia. Something she hadn't heard in those two years.

"It's Clara," she began.

"What?"

"Never mind. Not to you."

She stormed out.

The next week she filed for a divorce.

She served him papers.

"Why don't we have something to eat? At least talk... Maggie," he said over the phone.

"Fine," she said.

They went to a shabby little diner because she wouldn't have it any other way.

"Maggie," he said to her, "what is going on with you?"

"You're always with some bony broad..."

"Easy, Maggie. You left me."

"All I know is I found it exhilarating to be wanted after finding you with that Kensington woman."

Her mother tapped on the glass from across the dining room.

"I now know why she appears to me smoking…"

"Who?"

"Norma."

"Your mother appears to you? And smoking a cigarette?"

"She knows how much I hated when she was smoking."

"Okay, so why…"

"To tell me she hates what I'm doing."

In the moment Norma wasn't smoking. But walking, seemingly getting closer as if to reach for the door… and she tapped on the glass.

Clara got up to follow.

She too became an alternative identity following the death of her mother, during a time of passion.

And Magnolia Newman left the restaurant with a man who was no longer her husband, but she wondered if her mother would appear to her again because Clara Wood would take to her in any way she could.

But her mother turned the corner, and Clara braced the wall because her mother took Hunter Green by the hand.

Together they walked. Into the light. And vanished.

"Could I have another chance, Maggie?"

"Maybe." She was lost in reverie.

"Maybe we could start a little family…" he said, exiting the front door. "Do you see her now?"

"Nope," she said. "And maybe… just maybe…"

"I have so much to show you," he said.

"Please just take me to my cabin so I can sleep beside you in the dark and feel my way with you beneath the sheets." They ambled down the street.

They turned the corner.

"I yearn for being wanted in the most erotic way."

"Well in that regard, we're just two people who want to be wanted…"

And that evening they went home, back to their bedroom in New York, and in her mind, the cabin would remain the place of refuge where Hunter Green gave into her, and in that condo, Quinton did his best to give to her everything she desired.

Clara could never again feel the love she had for Hunter because the sex was raw, unmerciful, and she would yield to the passion of feeling something if even for only a moment.

Magnolia and Quinton Newman relished in the intimacy of another partner during their marriage. In the end they were exactly what each other wanted; and they left the restaurant knowing the secret obsession of Clara Wood, her alias, while in the cabin, was intimate passion.

And maybe, just maybe, she could have her way with him, and her mother would just stay if they had, in the mix of passion, a little family.

For once, Quinton Newman wasn't a bottom.

And when they were done...

Clara Wood smoked a cigarette.